A small town in Georgia. A family with a past. A trilogy packed with sensual secrets and private scandals!

Meet Tara McBride. She's always been a little straitlaced, unlike the rest of her scandalous family. That is, until Blake, a sexy-as-sin P.I., arrives on her doorstep. Suddenly she's on the run, dodging bullets and making wild, passionate love to Blake every night. She's having the time of her life. But can it last?

Savannah, Tara and Emily— the McBride Women. They've come home to put the past to rest. Little do they suspect what the future has in store for them!

SEDUCING SAVANNAH—
January 1998
TEMPTING TARA—
March 1998
ENTICING EMILY—
May 1998

Southern
SCANDALS

Dear Reader,

I've always believed that the only way to make the characters in my books come alive for my readers is for them first to come alive for me. And they do—sometimes so much it's a bit unnerving! They develop their own voices, their own quirks, their own hopes and anxieties. And by the time I finish telling their stories, they've become my friends.

Sometimes secondary characters become so real to me, I simply have to give them a story of their own. Blake, the hero in *Tempting Tara,* is one such character. He first appeared as a mysterious character in *Just Her Luck.* And then in *The Getaway Bride* he and the hero squared off against a madman. By the end of that book I was convinced that Blake needed a romance of his own. Tara McBride, with her outer strength and hidden insecurities, seemed to be the perfect match for him.

I hope you enjoy reading Tara and Blake's story. (For those of you who enjoy cameo appearances from past books, you might recognize some of Blake's friends in this story.) And don't forget to watch for *Enticing Emily,* the third book in my Southern Scandals trilogy, available in May 1998.

Happy reading,

Gina Wilkins

Gina Wilkins
TEMPTING TARA

Harlequin Books

TORONTO • NEW YORK • LONDON
AMSTERDAM • PARIS • SYDNEY • HAMBURG
STOCKHOLM • ATHENS • TOKYO • MILAN
MADRID • WARSAW • BUDAPEST • AUCKLAND

ISBN 0-373-25776-7

TEMPTING TARA

This edition published by arrangement with Harlequin Books S.A.

® and TM are trademarks of the publisher. Trademarks indicated with
® are registered in the United States Patent and Trademark Office, the
Canadian Trade Marks Office and in other countries.

Printed in U.S.A.

Prologue

TARA MCBRIDE didn't want to open the box. She really, really didn't want to open it.

Staring down at the shoebox-size plastic container in her hand, she thought of how smug she'd been when she'd packed it fifteen years ago. Not quite fourteen then, she'd already been an overachiever, someone who was destined to become a success at whatever she chose to do.

No one—least of all herself—would have believed that two months shy of her twenty-ninth birthday, she'd be washed up. A failure.

Fired.

The word echoed eerily in her mind. Since it had only happened yesterday, she was still trying to come to terms with it.

How oddly fitting that she'd had to come home to Honoria, Georgia to attend her uncle Josiah Jr.'s funeral this morning. A funeral seemed appropriate today. The end of her uncle's years of suffering. The end of Tara's career.

Fired.

She hadn't even told her family yet. She just couldn't admit—even to those who loved her—that she had failed so miserably.

"Come on, Tara," her twenty-six-year-old cousin

Emily urged, a matching plastic box clutched in her own hands. "Open your time capsule."

Time capsule. That was what the three cousins, Tara, Emily and Savannah McBride, had called it when they'd filled three plastic shoeboxes with mementos of their childhood, wrapped them in plastic garbage bags, stuffed them into an old cypress chest and buried them here in the woods behind Emily's house. They'd made a solemn promise that day to dig up the chest in fifteen years and read the letters they'd written to themselves, just to find out how many of their youthful dreams had come true.

It had sounded like fun at the time. Something to fill a lazy summer afternoon. Tara thought the time capsule had been Savannah's idea, but they'd all eagerly participated. In fact, those stupid letters had been Tara's suggestion. She'd been so naively, arrogantly certain that her brains and ambition would take her as far up any career ladder as she wanted to go. She'd had no idea what a mess her life would be in when she found that letter again.

Now Tara wished they'd just gone to see a movie that afternoon so long ago.

Stalling, she glanced at her cousins. Savannah, only a few weeks shy of her thirtieth birthday, and still as strikingly beautiful as she'd been as a teenager, didn't look much more enthusiastic than Tara felt about delving into the past. Only Emily looked as if she was rather enjoying this little adventure.

Tara supposed Emily would have welcomed any distraction this afternoon. It had been Emily's father they'd buried that morning, leaving Emily alone in a house full of troubling memories.

For Emily's sake, Tara tried to smile as she finally, reluctantly opened the box and sifted through the contents. The honors awards, the spelling-bee medals, the national test scores that had marked her as "gifted." And that letter to herself, detailing the high-powered career she had expected to be so well established in by now.

Bleakly, she stared into the box, and realized that she'd never had a dream that hadn't been planted in her head by the expectations of others. Now that she'd blown her chance at the impressive career everyone had predicted for her, she hadn't a clue what to do next. Not one dream of her own to pursue.

She had never felt so lost, so alone. And, for the first time in her life, she had a great many more questions than answers.

What was she going to do now?

1

TWO WEEKS LATER, on an afternoon in early June, Tara sat alone in her expensive, beautifully decorated Atlanta apartment—an apartment befitting a young attorney on the fast track to a partnership in an old and highly respected law firm. She took no pleasure in her surroundings; had she thought about it, she would have only worried about how she was going to pay the exorbitant rent now that she had no salary.

As she had nearly every day since she'd returned from Honoria, she huddled on the couch, a soap opera playing on the TV, cartons of uneaten Chinese food scattered on the coffee table in front of her. It was a gray, cloudy afternoon, but she hadn't turned on any lights. The heavy shadows suited her mood.

She had dressed that morning in a white T-shirt and baggy gray knit shorts, a pair of ratty white socks on her feet. Her white-blond hair fell to her shoulders, probably looking stringy since she hadn't bothered to style it. She wore no makeup. Her entire beauty regime for the past few days had consisted of brushing her teeth.

Her telephone rang occasionally, but she allowed the answering machine to pick it up. Her family thought she was away on business. Her few friends here in Atlanta, who knew the truth about her job, thought she was still in Honoria. She doubted anyone would suspect that she'd been holed up in her apartment all this time, slowly sinking into a depression she couldn't seem to climb out of.

She hated herself for behaving this way. Moping and sulking weren't her style. But then, she'd never been fired before. Never in her life had she truly failed at anything...and she couldn't seem to do anything now except sit in her apartment and ask herself what had gone wrong.

She'd tried to do the right thing—just as she'd always tried to follow the rules and make the right choices. All her life, she'd done what everyone wanted her to do—what everyone expected her to do—and she'd always been phenomenally successful. Yet, the first time she'd rebelled, the first time she'd refused to play by the rules, to go along with what was expected of her even when she honestly believed the others were wrong, she'd been summarily dismissed. Fired.

And now she didn't know what to do. Whose expectations to fulfill. Being fired for standing her own ground had made her wonder if she'd ever in her life done anything that hadn't been at someone else's bidding.

Her doorbell rang, once, then again. She ignored it.

A moment later, someone pounded on her door. She frowned and huddled more deeply into the corner of her couch.

The pounding didn't stop. It only got louder, more insistent.

Tara realized that the knocking had settled into a recognizable rhythm. "Shave and a haircut—two bits."

Over and over, until finally she jumped to her feet and stalked to the door, determined to send this annoying person on his way before he drove her nuttier than she'd already become.

Irritably, she jerked open the door without even pausing to see who was on the other side.

The man on her doorstep could have stepped out of a 1930's musical. From the gray felt fedora on his golden head to the snazzy black-and-white-checked suspenders he wore with a pale yellow shirt and loosely pleated charcoal slacks, he was obviously someone who followed no one's style except his own. Belying the urgency of his rapping on her door, he lounged on the doorstep as if he hadn't a care in the world. As if he'd had no doubt that she would get around to opening the door eventually.

"Oh, good. You're here." His smile was lazy, his eyes a wicked glint of bright blue beneath the shadow of his hat brim.

"Blake?" Tara felt her jaw drop. Though this man had been featured quite prominently in her fantasies during the past two years, he was the last person on earth she would have expected to find at her door this afternoon.

"Yeah. Listen, do you have any coffee? I haven't had any caffeine all day and I'm about to grow fangs. Instant would do in a pinch, but I really prefer fresh-brewed. It doesn't have to be anything fancy, just as long as it's hot and strong."

"I—er—" She lifted a hand to her temple, thinking maybe she'd fallen asleep on the sofa and was having a really bizarre dream. Bad Chinese food, maybe?

"Black. No sugar." Blake stepped past her as if he'd been warmly invited inside.

Tara found herself standing alone at the open door while he crossed her cluttered living room to take a seat in a wingback chair.

"Hey, *General Hospital*," he said, making himself comfortable in front of the TV. "Those Quartermaines are always in trouble, aren't they?"

"Blake, what are you—"

"If you've got any cookies to go with that coffee, I'd take a few. Don't go to any trouble, though, okay?"

She looked from Blake to the open doorway, wondering rather dazedly how he'd gotten through it. She couldn't believe he had just waltzed into her apartment and ordered coffee as if she was running a sidewalk café.

Tara had suffered from what she'd considered an embarrassingly juvenile crush on this man for almost two years, though she knew it was unlikely anything would come of it. They'd had no real connection. Blake had never been to her apartment before; there'd been no reason for him to stop by. He was only someone who had done some investigative work for the law firm where she'd been employed before she was—as always, she had to swallow hard before she finished the thought—fired.

She didn't even know his last name.

"Blake, this really isn't a good time for a visit," she said, suddenly uncomfortably aware of her appearance, and the condition of her usually impeccable apartment, as well as all the other reasons why she wasn't in the mood to entertain.

"I can see I caught you taking a lazy afternoon," he said sympathetically. "Everyone deserves one of those occasionally. I really hate to interrupt your day off, but there's something I need to discuss with you. We'll talk about it over coffee, shall we?"

It didn't look as though he was going anywhere until he told her why he'd come—and he seemed inclined to take his time about that. Tara sighed and closed the door with a fatalistic shrug.

Maybe she should have been more worried about having a strange man push his way into her house. But she wasn't afraid of Blake, even if she was curious about why he'd come. She had never heard anything negative about him from the management team at the law firm, and she, better than anyone, knew that they demanded only the highest standards from anyone affiliated with Carpathy, Dillon and Delacroix. In fact, she'd gotten the distinct impression that her former superiors had nothing but respect for Blake and his work.

She might as well give him coffee and find out what he was doing here.

"I'll, er, be right back," she said, running a hand through her rather limp hair.

He seemed to be interested in the soap opera. "No hurry," he assured her.

"Weird," she muttered as she walked into her kitchen and pulled open the cabinet door where she kept her coffee. "Definitely weird."

She wished now that she'd taken the trouble to put on a little makeup that morning.

WHEN SHE CARRIED a tray of coffee and cookies into the living room a few minutes later, Tara found Blake still absorbed in the drama taking place on her TV screen. He'd removed his hat, which now rested on the arm of his chair, and she could tell that he'd fluffed his dark golden hair by running his fingers through it. It tumbled onto his forehead, looking so good that Tara's mouth went dry. Unfortunately it also made her even more aware of how limp and lifeless her own must appear in contrast.

She had considered him an extremely attractive man since the first time she'd seen him at the law firm a couple of years ago. And he was, without a doubt, charming. He'd never failed to stop by her desk with a smile, a few bad jokes, some light flirtation.

Though she had always secretly looked forward to those infrequent visits, she'd made an effort to keep them in perspective, telling herself that it was okay to enjoy his attentions as long as she didn't make too much out of them. After all, Blake stopped by *everyone's* desk, not just hers. She'd known all along that she wasn't the type of woman a sexy, adventurous, footloose P.I. could be interested in.

And she most definitely did not want his pity now, if that was why he was here.

He glanced up and smiled when she entered the room, and he motioned toward the TV. "These people will never learn, will they? If you're going to tell a lie—make damned sure you don't get caught in it."

Tara lifted an eyebrow. "I'm not sure that's the moral lesson the writers were going for."

"Moral lesson? Tara, it's a soap opera."

"True." She set the tray on the coffee table as she

conceded his point, pushing aside cartons of congealed Chinese food to make room. "I, er, my apartment isn't usually this cluttered. I've been..."

He waved off her stammered explanation. "Don't sweat it. Housekeeping isn't high on my list when I'm taking time off work, either."

"I'm not exactly taking time off work. I was fired." Tara hated having to admit the humiliating truth, but she suspected that Blake, with his connections to her former law firm, already knew. How else would he have known to find her here on a weekday afternoon?

His mouth full of cookies, Blake waved his hand dismissively again. He swallowed before saying, "Vacation. Fired. What's the difference?"

She supposed he was trying to make her feel better. He wasn't.

"There's a very big difference," she said bitterly.

He shrugged. "The point is, you have some free time on your hands, right? Or have you already found a new position?"

"No, not yet." She hadn't even put out the first inquiry yet. The thought of having to admit to prospective employers that she'd been terminated from her last job because of her own obstinacy made her sick to her stomach.

Tara McBride had never had to beg for a job in her life. College scholarships, honors and awards, impressive offers of employment—they'd all come to her. She hadn't needed to ask.

She had never failed...until now.

"Great."

Blake's enthusiasm seemed rather callous. She frowned at him. "I'm glad you're so happy about it."

He chuckled. "I don't mean to sound insensitive. It's just that I need some help on a case, and I was hoping you would be free to give me a hand."

Tara wasn't sure she'd heard him correctly. "A case? You're kidding, right?"

"No." He took another sip from his mug. "You make great coffee. Did you bake these cookies? They're good."

"No, I got them at a bakery," she answered absently. "Blake, I'm not sure I understand. If you need clerical help, I'm really not..."

He shook his head. "I know you're way too over-qualified for that. I need you to do a bit of undercover work with me."

Now she *knew* she must have misunderstood him. Blake was a private investigator. She was a tax attorney—or at least, she had been until two weeks ago. How could she help him?

"Does this case involve tax fraud?" she hazarded.

"No. What bakery?"

She blinked. "What do you... Oh, the cookies. They came from Miller's Bakery, a couple of blocks from here."

He took another bite, then washed it down with more coffee. "Really good," he murmured appreciatively.

"Blake, try to stick with the conversation, will you?" she asked, losing patience. "Why did you come here?"

He set his coffee cup on the table, linked his hands in

front of him and leaned slightly toward her. "I need you, Tara McBride. Will you help me?"

LATER THAT EVENING, Blake stood once again at Tara's door, pleased with himself that he'd convinced her to go out with him that evening. It had been a spur-of-the-moment plan, and he was glad he'd pitched it as though he needed her to help him, rather than the other way around.

She definitely needed to get out, he'd decided after seeing her that afternoon. Though he'd managed to hide it, his first glimpse of her this afternoon had shaken him.

Blake had known Tara McBride for almost two years. He'd made it a point to spend a little time with her whenever he visited the offices of Carpathy, Dillon and Delacroix, her former law firm, and he'd always thought she was a beautiful woman with brains, ambition, determination, and a limitless future. From what he'd discreetly found out about her, he knew she'd been small-town-raised and Harvard-educated.

Way out of his league, in other words.

He'd never imagined he'd ever see her looking lost, vulnerable, frightened or defeated. Until today.

He'd told himself that the only reason he'd looked her up today was to make sure she was okay. He'd been shocked when he'd found out from the rather gossipy receptionist at the law firm that Tara had been summarily fired after a conflict with the senior partners. The receptionist had confided to Blake that Tara had left looking as though she'd "run smack into a brick wall." Carrying her belongings in her arms, she'd left without saying a word to anyone.

"I thought she was going to cry," the receptionist had whispered to Blake. "She didn't, but she looked like she might. I never thought I'd see Ms. McBride looking so devastated."

That had been two days ago. Blake had worried about Tara ever since, until finally he hadn't been able to resist seeing for himself that she was okay. He'd had a feeling that something was very wrong.

And when he saw her, he'd known that, once again, his instincts were on target.

She'd been resistant at first to going out with him. But she'd seemed intrigued by the idea of working with him on a case. Could it be that the buttoned-down attorney had been hiding a craving for adventure behind that gorgeous, corporate-clone facade? Blake could give her a taste—even if that was all he had to offer a woman like Tara McBride.

Wryly aware of how much he was anticipating spending the evening with her, he ran his right hand through his hair and reached out to press the doorbell.

The woman who opened the door to him this time bore little resemblance to the woebegone waif who'd greeted him earlier, he noted immediately. In her place was the poised, competent professional he'd known and admired—from afar—at the law firm.

She'd swept her shoulder-length, white-blond hair into a neat, firm twist at the back of her head. Her makeup was light, but skillfully applied. She wore a tailored black dinner suit with high-heeled black pumps. The fitted jacket came together in an intriguing, but tasteful V, and was fastened by glittery black buttons down the front. Deep pockets on the sides emphasized the curves of her slender hips. Her skirt was straight, and ended just above her knees, showcasing her long legs. Her jewelry consisted of diamond stud earrings, and a pearl choker clasped around her slender throat.

She was beautiful. And she represented everything that was missing from Blake's life.

Quickly shoving that unexpected insight to the back of his mind, he smiled and extended his left hand, in which he held a single, deep red rose in full bloom.

"This reminded me of you," he said. Classy, formal, stylized and beautiful, yet its bold coloring hinted at passion in the same way Tara's glittering, blue-violet eyes had often made Blake wonder what secrets lay behind her polished facade.

He made sure his fingers brushed hers when she reached out to accept the bloom. The all-too-brief contact jolted Blake, who was immediately hit with an urge to pull her into his arms.

Careful, son. That's not what this evening is about.

This evening was for Tara, not for Blake. And he would do well to keep that in mind.

CHARMED against her better judgment, Tara couldn't help lifting the fragrant flower to her nose. It was a nice gesture on Blake's part, she thought a bit wistfully, but she found it hard to believe this lusciously ostentatious rose had reminded him of her. A white rose, maybe, or a cool lavender orchid. But nothing as bold and splashy as this gorgeous bloom.

"Thank you," she said, making an effort to keep her voice steady and assured. "I'll put this in water and then I'm ready to go. Unless you'd like something to drink first?"

He shook his head. "No. But thanks."

It had occurred to her as she'd dressed for dinner that this was the first time in two weeks that she'd actually looked forward to getting out of her apartment. The fact that she was going out with Blake—well, that certainly added to her anticipation. But it wasn't only that.

She was tired of sitting alone, moping. She'd had two weeks to get that out of her system, but now it was time to get on with her life...even if she had no idea what she would do next.

She'd always been a fighter—which was part of the reason she no longer had a job. It was time for her to start fighting depression and get back on her feet.

She had nearly lost all that newfound confidence again when she'd opened the door and seen Blake. He looked...gorgeous, she thought with an inward sigh. He was wearing a loosely constructed, silvery-gray suit with a crisp white shirt and a blue-and-silver patterned silk tie. He'd left off the fedora this time, and his dark-gold hair was brushed into a sexy, disheveled style that made her itch to run her fingers through it.

He was spectacular, and—as much as she would like to believe otherwise—completely wrong for her. He was dashing, exciting, eccentric and unpredictable— things Tara might have always secretly wished to be, but wasn't. She was about as exciting as...as...well, as the tax codes she spent so much time studying, she thought with another hidden sigh. She really couldn't fathom why Blake had bothered to look her up.

After putting the rose in a crystal bud vase, Tara picked up the slim black purse she'd packed for the evening, took a deep, calming breath and turned to Blake, who was watching her with a bit too much perception behind that deceptively lazy smile of his.

In a courtly, old-fashioned gesture, he offered his arm. "Shall we?"

Tonight is only business, Tara reminded herself. *We'll have dinner, he'll make his pitch, I'll turn it down, and then send him on his way.*

But there was no reason she couldn't enjoy the evening while it lasted, was there? She smiled and took his arm.

Their smiles faded as both of them looked down at her fingers curled around his forearm. He felt surprisingly strong beneath the loose fabric of his jacket, suggesting that his slender physique was a bit misleading. She looked up, only to find him gazing into her eyes, and she suddenly realized how very close they were standing.

She cleared her throat. "I'm ready when you are."

This time his smile was purely sinful. "Sweetheart—I'm *past* ready."

Still trying to decide how to respond, she allowed him to tow her out of the apartment and into the beautiful spring evening.

"AN ART GALLERY? We're having dinner at an art gallery?" Tara looked at Blake in confusion when he turned the car in to the already crowded lot of the exclusive Buckhead establishment.

Though there were available spaces much closer to the door, Blake chose a parking space just inside the entrance to the parking lot. Tara thought it was a little strange but assumed he just wanted a space close to the exit, so he wouldn't get hemmed in when they were ready to leave.

After he'd turned off the car's engine Blake smiled at Tara. "Actually, we're having dinner later. We're here now because of the case I told you about."

She felt her eyes widen. "The case? You mean, you're working *now*? And I'm here to help?"

He nodded. "Yeah. And I can't tell you how much I appreciate it."

"But, Blake, I—"

He opened his door, cutting off her arguments that she'd never agreed to this and that she wasn't qualified to assist a P.I. in any assignment, regardless of what it might be. Her only expertise was in tax law. But he rounded the front of his sleek black sports car, opened her door, and helped her out before she could manage to ask him to take her home.

"I don't even know what you want me to do," she murmured to him as he drew her inexorably toward the gallery doors.

"Smile and look beautiful," he advised her casually, then nodded genially at a wealthy-looking middle-aged couple who reached the doors at the same time.

Tara swallowed hard and tried to smile.

A rather intimidating man with a clipboard stood at the entrance to the crowded gallery. "Name?"

"Bill Austin," Blake supplied smoothly, then smiled at Tara. "And guest."

The guard glanced at the list, nodded, and scrawled a check mark on the page. "Have a nice time," he said, waving them in.

"I didn't know your last name was Austin," Tara whispered as they entered the room full of interesting-looking, fashionably dressed guests.

"It isn't," he replied quietly, snagging a glass of champagne from a conveniently located table. He offered it to Tara, who took it automatically as she tried to figure out what on earth was going on.

"Look over here, darling," he said a bit more loudly, guiding her toward an easel on which stood the most incredibly ugly painting Tara had ever seen. "Isn't this breathtaking?"

"It certainly is," she muttered, trying to find anything at all of interest in the muddy swirls of green, brown and yellow. "Looks like something you'd find on the floor of a barn. I'm surprised there aren't any flies buzzing around it."

Keeping his eyes fixed on the canvas, Blake cleared his throat. There was just the slightest quiver in his voice when he asked brightly, "Wouldn't you love the opportunity to own a genuine McCauley painting?"

She cocked her head. "If this is a McCauley, I'd just as soon have an Elvis on black velvet. With sequins," she added, making sure no one but Blake could hear her.

Blake took her totally by surprise when he bent his head and pressed a quick, firm kiss against her lips.

"I knew you'd be as enthusiastic about it as I am," he

said as he drew away. While his tone was innocuous enough, his bright blue eyes gleamed with what might have been amusement.

Tara struggled to remember how to breathe again. She certainly didn't want Blake to know that his brief, impulsive kiss had set her pulse racing.

A short, portly man in a bad toupee approached them with a beaming smile. "Spectacular, isn't it?" he asked, nodding toward the canvas.

"Incredible," Blake replied.

The man looked at Tara expectantly.

"I...er...I've never seen anything like it," she answered candidly.

Blake slipped an arm around her waist. "We were just talking about the power of it. All that barely suppressed emotion."

The little man nodded with such enthusiasm that Tara couldn't help watching to see if his toupee would remain in place. It did.

"This painting would be a valuable addition to any private collection," he hinted broadly.

Blake nodded gravely. "I'm sure it would. But, of course, my wife and I would like to look at everything before we make our selection."

Tara tried not to react to the news of her matrimonial status, but she was afraid she wasn't nearly as good at this kind of thing as Blake was. It would help, she thought irritably, if she knew what the hell they were doing here.

"Of course," the man said. "Please, enjoy yourselves. If there's anything I can do to help you, my name is Botkin."

And then he started to walk away—probably looking for another sucker, Tara decided. She turned to Blake, hoping for some explanation. But before she could ask, she blinked in astonishment. The little man had given her a familiar pat on the butt as he brushed past her! There was no way to believe it had just been an accidental touch—Botkin's hand had slid around her side and lingered long enough to leave her in no doubt that she'd just been felt up.

Of all the nerve! she thought, turning to glare at him as he hurried away. And she'd expected this would be a classy function.

"Blake," she began, turning purposefully toward him again.

Her "husband" tightened his hold on her waist and urged her toward the next painting, dodging people along the way, effectively preventing Tara from asking any questions.

They spent the next half hour moving from one painting to another, sipping champagne and pretending to study them all. Tara found only one among the group that she didn't actually hate, and her comments to Blake, murmured for his ears only, grew increasingly acerbic.

"Doesn't this place carry anything by Norman Rockwell?" she finally asked in exasperation, glaring at another example of muddy colors run amok.

Blake laughed. "Darling, I'm glad you talked me into coming tonight. I'm having such a good time."

"I'm so happy to hear that," she returned sweetly.

The funny thing was that she was actually having a good time, too, she thought in bemusement.

She must really have been hard up for entertainment lately.

She was hardly even surprised when Blake glanced at his watch, then turned to her and said, "Of course, dear. The ladies' room is in the back of the gallery, I believe."

Obviously, Blake wanted her to go to the ladies' room. She didn't know why, but what the heck. She hadn't known what he wanted from her all evening. So, she would go to the ladies' room.

Blake gallantly escorted her to the back of the gallery, through a rabbit warren of hallways and showrooms. Either he spent a lot of time here, or he'd memorized a floor plan, because he never hesitated. He nodded toward a door bearing a discreet brass plaque that said Ladies.

"Take your time, sweetheart," he urged her. "I'll make a quick trip into the men's room and then meet you back here, all right?"

Thinking that this was all very strange, Tara nodded and pushed open the door to the ladies' room.

There was no one in the elegantly appointed lounge area. Tara drifted to the large mirror that dominated one wall, set her purse on the counter and checked her reflection. She looked more like herself than she had in the past two weeks, she thought with faint satisfaction. There was actually a bit of color in her face again...left there, she had no doubt, by that brief yet memorable kiss.

After refreshing her lipstick, she picked up her purse, pushed open the door and peered out into the hallway. It was empty.

Stepping through the door, she hesitated, wondering if she should go back to the main gallery or wait where she was for Blake. It was rather eerie being in this back hallway alone, even knowing that so many people were gathered nearby. Didn't any of these glittering, artsy-type women ever need to...

A sound from a room just down the hall made her turn in that direction.

"Blake?" she whispered. "Is that you?"

A loud thump came from the room. It sounded to Tara's suddenly active imagination like a body hitting the floor. She swallowed, telling herself she was being ridiculous. She was in an art gallery, for heaven's sake.

Lifting her chin and wrapping herself in the courage she'd developed through years of battling the IRS for her clients, she moved toward the open doorway of the room from which she'd heard the odd noises. If she didn't find Blake there, she would assume he'd gone into the gallery without her.

The first thing she saw when she stepped into what appeared to be a private office was the body lying on the floor.

To her horror, Tara recognized the portly little man with the toupee, the one who'd approached her and Blake earlier at the McCauley painting. Botkin's formerly florid face was now bleached of color, his toupee knocked askew so that it barely covered his balding scalp. The front of his once pristine white shirt was now stained red.

Instinctively, Tara dropped her purse and knelt beside him. "Can you hear me?"

He groped weakly at her jacket with one pudgy

hand, tugging at the fabric. His mouth moved as if he were trying to speak, but nothing emerged except a ragged groan.

"Don't try to talk," Tara advised him urgently. "I'll get help."

"They knew..." he gasped. "The paintings were..."

The man's hand fell heavily to the floor. His eyes rolled back. A chill crawled down Tara's spine, along with a horrible suspicion that she had just watched a man die.

Her stomach lurched. She surged to her feet, her mouth open to scream for help.

Two very large, very strong arms came around her from behind, and before she could react, she found herself pinned against someone big, solid, and unmistakably menacing.

2

A HEAVY HAND covered Tara's mouth before she could cry out. She resisted automatically, futilely struggling to break free from the man's shackling arms.

"Who the hell are you?" a gravelly voice demanded in her ear. "And what are you doing here? What did he say to you?"

She managed to turn her head and look him straight in the face. She memorized his features in one searching glance before he cursed and turned her head away from him again.

"I guess it doesn't matter what he said," her attacker muttered. "You won't be telling anybody."

She couldn't breathe. His massive hand covered her nose as well as her mouth, effectively blocking her air. Her vision started to blur. Tara clawed at his hand, but he hardly seemed to notice her frantic movements.

Silently, she screamed Blake's name.

Someone rushed at them from behind. She heard something solid smash against the head of the man holding her. He fell like a boulder, nearly taking her down with him.

Steadying hands caught her arms. "Are you all right?" Blake demanded, holding her on her feet.

Gasping for breath, she nodded. "What—?"

The sound of running footsteps made Blake stiffen.

"Let's go," he said, pushing Tara somewhat roughly toward the door. "Now!"

"But..."

"Tara, *move.*"

Something in his voice made her respond without further argument. She allowed him to take her hand and pull her out of the office. A man in a dark suit stood at the left end of the hallway, blocking their path to the main gallery. He held something shiny in his hand.

Blake turned right, almost dragging Tara after him as he ran down the hallway and through another office. He shoved open a door, which led outside to an alley.

"Blake—"

He didn't hesitate. "Run!"

Stumbling in her high heels, Tara tried to keep up with him. Something hit the wall of the building next door to the gallery. A shard of brick seemed to explode from the wall, missing Tara's cheek by inches.

Blake cursed and yanked at her arm. "Hurry!"

Tara told herself it couldn't possibly have been a bullet. She tried to convince herself that she'd watched entirely too much television during the past two weeks. But the urgency in Blake's voice and the cold fear in her own chest propelled her to run faster.

They rounded the front of the gallery, emerging in the parking lot, which was crowded with vehicles and people either arriving late to the art show or leaving early. Never slowing down, Blake zigzagged through the obstacles toward his own car. He unlocked the doors with a remote device and had the engine run-

ning and the car in gear almost before Tara had
crawled into the passenger seat.

He pulled out of the parking lot with a burst of
speed, just missing a black Lexus that was turning in at
the same time and a BMW coming from the other direction. Tara closed her eyes tightly as horns blew and
tires squealed. She felt the back of Blake's car fishtail
for a moment, but he steadied it almost immediately
and sped away from the gallery.

"We're being followed," he said before Tara could
catch her breath to demand explanations. "Fasten your
seat belt and hang on."

She obeyed his curt instructions with shaking hands.
She didn't dare ask what would happen if whoever
was following them actually caught up with them.

IT TOOK BLAKE less than five miles to lose their pursuers. Driving through a neighborhood of built-to-
impress mansions in one of the more exclusive Buckhead neighborhoods, he checked the rearview mirror
repeatedly, until he was finally satisfied that he'd
eluded the other car. Only then did he turn his attention to Tara, who'd been sitting in absolute silence, her
hands twisted in her lap as she waited for an explanation.

He wished he had one to offer her. He had no idea
how a case that was supposed to be so simple, so safe,
had gone so very wrong. His assignment had been
simply to accept an envelope of information from an
anonymous contact. If he'd had any inkling that there
would be danger involved, he never would have invited Tara to go with him.

"Are you all right?" he asked, reliving the shock of finding her struggling for her life in that back office, a dead man at her feet.

She countered with a question of her own. "Are they still chasing us?"

"We've lost them," he assured her.

She nodded, though she didn't look particularly relieved. "Will you please take me home now?" she asked, her tone just a bit too polite.

Blake winced. "I wish I could."

Tara gave him a look that he suspected had made hardened IRS agents quail on occasion. "What do you mean? Why can't you take me home?"

"Where's your purse, Tara?" he asked gently.

"I...er..." She looked around for a moment, then grimaced. "I dropped it. When I saw that man lying on the floor."

Blake nodded. "That's what I figured. The guy who grabbed you must have fallen on it when I hit him with the bronze."

She swallowed. "Did you... Was he...?"

He understood what she was trying to ask. "I didn't kill him. Probably just stunned him."

In fact, the guy had probably been in the car that had followed them out of the gallery parking lot.

Tara drew a shaky breath of relief. "Thank God."

Blake thought it best not to tell her that his first instinct, when he'd seen the jerk with his hands on Tara, obviously hurting her, had been to kill. The fury that had crashed through him had been powerful and violent. And since Blake didn't consider himself a violent man, that had shaken him.

"They have your purse," he said grimly, turning to more immediate concerns. "Which means they have your address, and even your keys. If we go to your apartment now, someone will likely be there waiting for us."

"Someone?" Tara's voice had gotten higher, tighter. "*Someone* will be at my apartment, waiting for us? Can you be a little more specific?"

He made another sharp turn, checked the rearview mirror again, then tried to answer her. "I'm afraid I'm a little short on details right now. Trust me, Tara, I have no more idea of what's going on than you do. This was supposed to be a safe, easy assignment. Something went wrong."

"Obviously," Tara retorted with heavy sarcasm. "Someone tried to *shoot* us!"

He remembered the sound of a silenced bullet striking brick, only inches from Tara's face, and his anger threatened to choke him again. But he managed to speak fairly normally when he said, "I'm afraid so."

He turned onto an entrance ramp for I-75, headed northwest—the opposite direction from Tara's apartment.

"Where are we going?" she demanded.

"Somewhere safe," he replied. "Someplace where we can talk."

"Who are they, Blake? The man who was lying on the floor of that office. The man who grabbed me. The one who shot at us. What do they all have to do with your case?"

He didn't know. And he knew she would find no reassurance in his ignorance. "We can talk more easily when I don't have to concentrate on my driving," he said, taking the easy way out.

Taking the hint, she fell quiet. But he knew his respite would be a brief one.

BLAKE TOOK TARA to a little motel in Marietta. The place was old, probably built in the early fifties, and the "rooms" consisted of individual small stucco cabins clustered around the office in the center. The paint was faded and peeling, and all the windows needed a good cleaning, but at least the motel didn't seem to be in danger of imminent condemnation.

Blake didn't bother to stop at the office, but pulled into a parking space in front of the cabin farthest from the others, at the very back of the compound. He slipped a key from his pocket and nodded toward the cabin door. "We'll be safe here while I make some calls," he said.

Tara looked doubtfully from Blake to the secluded motel cabin. He expected her to go inside with him, a man she hardly knew, after all that had happened to her because of him?

He shot her a quick glance. "Surely you know that you're perfectly safe with me."

No, as a matter of fact, she didn't know that. Because of him, she'd been at the wrong end of a gun for the first time in her life. "I want to know what's going on."

"So do I," he answered grimly. "But we aren't going to get any answers sitting out here in the car. Trust me, Tara."

She bit her lip as she considered all her options. All

the reasons she *shouldn't* trust him, considering everything. And then she reached for the door handle.

Maybe she was making a big mistake listening to him, trusting him at least a little...but it wouldn't be the first mistake she'd made in the past few weeks.

The room was surprisingly clean. A double bed took up most of the floor space. In front of the single window sat a round table with two chairs. A long dresser was pushed up against the opposite wall, a small TV bolted to one end of it. A door at the back of the room probably led into the bathroom.

"This is where you've been staying?" Tara was a bit surprised that Blake, with his expensive-looking car and wardrobe, would choose such modest accommodations.

"Occasionally," he answered with a shrug. "Are you hungry?"

She stared at him, wondering how he could possibly think she was hungry, under the circumstances. And then she scowled, wondering how she could possibly *be* hungry, under the circumstances. Because she was.

"A little," she admitted.

"Me, too. There's some food in the other room. Want to grab something for us while I make a call?"

He was acting as if they'd simply stopped off here for a snack after a pleasant outing at an art gallery, Tara thought in amazement as she watched him perch on the edge of the bed and reach for the telephone on the single nightstand. She wondered if being shot at was commonplace for this enigmatic P.I. She wasn't feeling nearly as calm about it as he looked. But then, she supposed it wouldn't do any good for both of them to fall to pieces.

Trying to emulate his composure, she opened the door at the back of the room to find an unexpectedly roomy dressing area that led into the bathroom. A small refrigerator sat beneath the counter. Opening it, she found soft drinks and fruit juices, a package of lunch meat, cheese, mustard, bread, a jar of pickles and another of olives. A basket on the counter above the refrigerator held bags of chips and dried fruit, individually packaged pastries, paper plates and plastic cutlery.

This wasn't exactly what she'd had in mind when she'd agreed to have dinner with Blake, Tara thought with a sigh.

She gathered a few things to make a sandwich and carried them to the table in the other room. Blake hung up the phone just as she walked in.

"No answer," he muttered.

"Who were you trying to call?"

"Information." Without looking at her, he started dialing again.

Tara set to work making dinner, though most of her attention was on Blake, who seemed to be having no success reaching anyone by telephone. He finally slammed the receiver down with a muttered curse, and sat for a moment gazing into space, obviously lost in thought.

Tara couldn't help staring at him. He seemed so different from the man she'd known at the law firm. She'd never seen him without his lazy grin, or a mischievous glint in his bright blue eyes. With his laid-back manner and light-colored, loose-fitting clothes, she'd always considered him the antithesis of the grim-faced, steely-eyed private investigator of fiction. She'd certainly never thought of him as tough or dangerous.

Looking at him now, she rapidly revised that innocuous mental image. Something in his expression made her pulse race a bit faster. She told herself it was only nerves.

He glanced her way, and she watched him make a deliberate effort to summon one of his easy smiles. But it was too late—she would never view him in quite the same way as she had before. She'd seen the menace in him when he'd taken out the big man who'd grabbed her, and the determination in him when he'd all but dragged her to his car and then efficiently evaded the men who'd pursued them from the gallery.

She knew now that there was much more to Blake than the smiling charmer she'd known on and off for the past couple of years.

"You—er—can't reach your client?" she asked.

"No. The number he gave me has been disconnected."

"What's going on, Blake?"

He sighed. "I don't know."

That wasn't the answer she wanted to hear.

He picked up the phone again.

"Who are you calling now? The police?" she asked hopefully.

"No. Not yet. What's your phone number, Tara?"

"*My* number?"

He nodded patiently, his finger hovering above the number pad.

Though she couldn't imagine why he wanted to hear her answering machine, she recited the number for him.

He dialed it, waited a moment, then scowled and slammed the receiver into the cradle. "Damn."

"What?" she asked warily.

His eyes held an apology when he answered. "A man answered."

She went cold. A strange man was in her apartment, going through her things, rummaging through her life, monitoring her calls. The feeling of invasion was sickening.

"Call the police," she insisted. "Tell them there's someone in my apartment who has no right to be there. Damn it, Blake, do something!"

He stood and caught her forearms in his hands, looking steadily into her eyes. "Calm down."

"Calm down? *Calm down?*" She gaped at him in disbelief. "We were supposed to be going out for dinner. That's all, dinner. And now a man has been shot, someone grabbed me and tried to smother me, someone else tried to shoot us, and we're stuck hiding out in this dingy motel in Marietta while some strange guy helps himself to whatever he wants in my apartment. You tell me that you don't know what's going on, but you won't call the police. And you want me to calm down?"

"It was only a suggestion," he answered mildly. "Feel free to get hysterical if it will make you feel better."

That brought her chin up. "I'm not going to get hysterical."

"Good choice."

"Don't start patronizing me, Blake," she warned him quietly. "Considering everything, I think I've handled this evening very well."

"Tara, you've handled this evening beautifully, considering everything. And I'm not patronizing you. I'm trying to apologize for getting you into this mess in the first place."

His blue eyes turned dark with self-recrimination. "If I'd had any suspicion that things would go this badly, I'd never have taken you with me to the art gallery. All I was supposed to do was to meet someone in the men's room, accept an envelope from him, and then leave. I thought you could provide me with a good cover during the evening, make me look less suspicious for being there, and then we could have a nice dinner afterward. I never anticipated the rest of this."

For some reason, she believed him.

"Was the man with the toupee the one you were supposed to meet?" she asked. "The one named Botkin?"

Blake grimaced. "I really hate to keep saying this, but...I don't know. My guess would be that he was."

"What...?"

Blake interrupted her next question. "Why don't we eat our sandwiches and I'll tell you what I know so far? And then I'll try again to find out what the hell went wrong."

She nodded. "All right. What do you want to drink?"

His smile was a bit crooked. "A double bourbon, but

I'll settle for a cola. Sit down, I'll get it. What would you like?''

"I saw some single-serving cans of orange juice. I'd like one of those, please." Considering how jittery she was already, Tara didn't think caffeine was a good idea.

Blake nodded and headed for the refrigerator while Tara set their dinner of sandwiches, pickles and chips on the small, round table. The drapes were closed over the window beside the table, giving an illusion of intimacy within the little cottage.

They took their seats and opened their drinks. Blake looked glumly at his plate. "I was going to take you someplace really nice," he murmured ruefully. "I had rather hoped to impress you this evening."

"Well, you've certainly made an impression," she responded, her tone dry.

He winced. "Not exactly the one I had in mind."

She picked up her sandwich. "Tell me about your case."

Between bites, Blake filled her in.

"I got a call from someone in an insurance company I work for sometimes—the same way I occasionally conduct investigations for your law firm," he began.

"Former law firm," Tara muttered.

He nodded. "Anyway, the person who called me wasn't my usual contact, but since I don't always talk to the same person, I didn't find anything odd about that."

"You said he asked you to meet someone at the art gallery and pick up an envelope?"

Instead of directly answering her, Blake asked a

question of his own. "You've heard of C. Jackson Will-fort?"

"Of course. Who hasn't heard of him?"

The billionaire industrialist was a prominent figure in Georgia society, parlaying old family money into a lavish, high-profile life-style. He had a luxurious condo in Atlanta and an opulent, fortress-like compound outside of Savannah, and was almost as well known for the parties he threw as for his outspoken conservative political views and his generous philanthropy.

As Willfort approached his fiftieth birthday, there had been rumors that he was considering a run for office—governor, perhaps, or senator. Tara had even heard whispers that he was eyeing the Oval Office.

"You know that he's an avid art collector?"

She nodded. "Didn't he have some valuable paintings stolen from his collection recently?"

"Yeah. There was a break-in at the apartment he keeps close to his office in downtown Atlanta. Some cash, jewelry and silver was stolen, along with several paintings that he had intended to place on display in the lobby of a local bank. It was the first time Willfort had ever announced plans to share any of his private art collection with the public, so it got some attention. Apparently, someone found out the paintings were being stored at the apartment and managed to get to them."

Tara frowned. "But wouldn't there have been heavy security in an apartment that contained cash, jewelry, silver and art?"

"There was. A guard was seriously wounded, almost killed. It looked like a professional job."

"An inside job, maybe?" Tara hazarded, thinking of all the TV she'd watched during the past two weeks.

Blake shrugged. "That's always a possibility."

"The insurance company you're working for—did they carry the policy for the items that were taken?"

"Yes. I'm often called in for big claims like this, either to try to recover the merchandise or to make sure no insurance fraud is involved. All I was told this time was that someone who works for the Pryce Gallery— someone who was afraid to give his name or come out publicly—had some information concerning the robbery. As I've already told you, I was to meet him in the men's room, where he would give me an envelope and then discreetly disappear. I was to leave the gallery, check the contents of the envelope to see if it contained anything of interest, and then get back to my client at the number he gave me. Quick. Simple. Safe—or so I thought. But no one showed up in the men's room, and when I went back to collect you...well, you know what happened then."

"So what went wrong?"

He shoved a hand through his hair. "I wish to hell I knew."

"Why aren't you calling the police?" She finally asked the question that had been bothering her the most. Every time she'd mentioned the police, Blake's expression had grown shuttered. She wanted to know why.

Again, Blake's eyes shifted away from hers. He

glanced at his watch, then reached for the television remote that lay on the nightstand beside the telephone.

"You're going to watch TV?" Tara asked in disbelief. "Now?"

"I want to check the local news," he replied, pressing the power button. "Before we call the police, it might be a good idea to see what's being said about tonight's events."

Tara tried to be patient as he concentrated on the unfolding news report. Several national stories took the lead, and then both Blake and Tara tensed as the news anchor mentioned a robbery at a local art gallery that evening. Cash and a collection of valuable framed miniatures that had been stored in a back office for an upcoming show were missing.

"Details are still sketchy," the anchorwoman recited, "but police are searching for a man and woman, both blond, both believed to be in their early thirties, who attended the showing this evening as Mr. and Mrs. Bill Austin. If anyone has any information regarding this robbery, they are asked to call the Atlanta police department."

Tara spun in her chair to stare at Blake. "The police are looking for *us*? But what about the man who was killed? And why didn't they mention my real name, since they know who I am?"

"I don't think the police have as many details about what went on there as we do," Blake replied.

"You mean they don't know someone was murdered at that gallery tonight?"

He nodded.

Tara sprang to her feet, moving toward the telephone. "Blake, we have to tell someone. We *saw* him. We're witnesses."

Blake stood, blocking her way. "We're suspects."

His blunt words made her catch her breath. She shook her head slowly. "No one would believe we had anything to do with this."

"We were there, under assumed names. We were wandering around in the back of the gallery during the show. I'm quite sure there are a couple of loyal gallery employees who would be willing to swear they saw us coming out of that office. The same loyal employees who tried to put a bullet into us earlier."

"But you're a private investigator. You were there on a case. And I'm an attorney—or at least, I was until..."

She bit her lip. Having been recently fired by her law firm didn't exactly provide a glowing character reference.

"In general, police officers aren't all that fond of private investigators," Blake murmured. "And at the moment, I can't reach my client to prove that I *was* there on a case. I have a few friends on the force, but I'd rather wait until we have more to go on before I risk getting us hauled in for interrogation."

"What aren't you telling me, Blake?"

He shook his head. "There's nothing specific," he assured her. "I just...well, I have a feeling."

She lifted an eyebrow. "A feeling?"

She would almost have sworn that his cheeks darkened as he cleared his throat and looked away. "Sometimes I just know when something's all wrong. And I've been hearing all kinds of mental warning bells about this mess, ever since I found out the number I was given isn't a working number."

Narrowing her eyes, she searched his face. "You're saying that you're...what? Psychic?"

He scowled. "Let's just say I've learned to trust my instincts."

"And your instincts are telling you not to call the police."

"Yeah."

He looked at her squarely. "I don't know what's going on, Tara, and I'm sorry as hell that I've gotten you involved in it. I know you think we should call the police, tell them what happened, and let them take care of everything. If that's what you really want me to do, I'll call and we'll take our chances."

"But your instincts...or your funny feelings, or whatever you call them, tell you that would be a mistake," she finished slowly.

Still holding her gaze with his, Blake nodded.

She drew a ragged breath. "You've had a lot more experience with this sort of thing than I have," she said after a long pause. "Do what you think is best."

To her surprise, he bent his head and pressed a quick, hard kiss against her mouth.

"Thank you," he murmured. "For trusting me."

He was going to have to stop doing that, Tara mused as Blake moved away. For some strange reason, her mind simply stopped functioning when his lips touched hers.

Blake picked up the phone and punched in a number. Tara watched and listened as he identified himself to someone on the other end.

"It's Blake," he said without bothering to add a surname. "I need you to do something for me."

Whoever it was he was talking to apparently agreed without hesitation.

As Blake continued giving instructions, Tara found herself wondering if anyone ever denied this man anything.

The fact that she was here in this room with him, involved in something that made no sense at all to her, was proof that he was extremely persuasive. She was going to have to be on her guard to make sure that he didn't talk her into a great deal more than she could handle.

3

TARA WAITED until Blake hung up the phone before asking, "What are we going to do now?"

He smiled at her, obviously trying to reassure her. "We can wait here for a while longer. We should be..."

His smile faded. He turned his head suddenly toward the window, like an animal that had just caught a faint whiff of danger.

"What is it?" she asked, her own instincts going on alert.

It seemed that she, too, was beginning to trust in Blake's "feelings."

He moved swiftly across the room and shifted the curtain just enough to allow him to glance out into the parking lot.

"We have to go," he said, dropping the curtain back into place. "Now."

Tara's heart tripped as Blake took her hand in an urgent grip. "What did you see out there?"

"The same car that was following us earlier. It just cruised past my car. We're about to have company we don't want." Blake was moving toward the bathroom as he talked, pulling her after him.

"How did they know to come here?" she whispered, as if their pursuers could hear through the walls.

"I don't—oh, hell."

She eyed him warily. "What?"

"You have caller I.D. at your apartment."

It wasn't a question, but she nodded, anyway. "Yes."

He hissed a curse through his teeth, apparently directed at himself. And then he pulled at her hand again. "Come on. We're going out the window."

"How are we going to get to your car?" she asked.

Blake already had the window open in the old-fashioned bathroom. He'd left the light off and Tara could see that there was nothing behind the little cabin but an empty lot filled with thigh-high weeds, scraggly bushes and a few trees. Beyond that was what appeared to be a rundown used-car lot, now closed for the night.

Without pausing to answer her question, Blake turned to boost Tara out the window. She hiked the slim-fitting skirt of her black dinner suit high up on her thighs, telling herself this was no time to worry about modesty. She doubted that Blake was interested in gawking at her legs when they had much more serious matters to concern them.

Blake slipped through the opening with far more dexterity than Tara. The minute his feet touched the ground, he was on the move again, headed for the empty lot. Tara clutched his hand and stayed very close to his side, half expecting to hear a shout or a gunshot from the cabin behind them.

The weeds and bushes tore at her hose, and she stumbled across the uneven ground in her heeled pumps. Blake steadied her, murmuring something encouraging. He seemed to be headed toward the car lot.

She followed him mutely, trusting him to know what he was doing.

Her heart was pounding, her pulse racing. She told herself it was fear—but she was also aware of an underlying exhilaration that startled her. She was a tax attorney, for Pete's sake, not one of those dashing secret-agent types from the movies!

Keeping low, and urging her to do the same, Blake zigzagged through the collection of rather dilapidated vehicles until he reached a black pickup truck that looked somewhat better than the rest of the lot. Tara was startled when Blake pulled his key ring out of his pocket and shoved a key into the lock of the driver's door.

"Get in," he said, motioning for her to climb in and scoot over.

She did.

As Blake started the engine and shifted into drive, Tara saw a light go on in the bathroom of the cabin they'd just deserted. A dark figure was silhouetted against the window for a moment, and then Blake pulled out of the car lot and accelerated, leaving the motel—and his sports car—behind them.

They were on the road for well over an hour, driving a circuitous route that finally took them into Carrollton, some forty miles southwest of Atlanta. Blake explained briefly that he didn't want to get too far out of the area, and that was just about the extent of their conversation during that drive. Blake seemed lost in thought, and Tara was too busy trying to make sense of the evening to attempt to draw answers out of him.

Blake pulled into a service station and parked at the

side, next to a door marked Men. He reached into the storage area behind the seat. Tugging a duffel bag into his lap, he opened his door.

"I'll be right back," he said. "Lock the doors."

That was one instruction he didn't need to repeat. She had the doors locked almost before Blake had climbed out of the truck.

She didn't recognize the lanky cowboy who approached the driver's door a few minutes later. He was wearing snug jeans, a white, long-sleeved western-cut shirt, boots and a black hat pulled low over his face. Even his walk was different, a slightly bowlegged amble that drew her eyes to his slim, rolling hips.

Only the duffel bag beneath his arm looked familiar.

Blake tapped on the driver's window for her to unlock the door.

"I should make you say 'trick or treat' before you get in," she muttered as she opened the door for him.

He chuckled. "The suit matched the sports car," he explained. "A pickup truck calls for an image change."

He tossed the duffel bag over the seat and slid behind the wheel. His hat almost touched the top of the cab; he tugged it off and laid it on the seat between them.

"Don't touch my hat," he warned in a broad Texas drawl. "That was my great-granddaddy's hat. I wouldn't want nothing to happen to it."

She looked up from pulling a burr off her tattered hose. "Don't worry about your hat. It's your throat I'm going for if this evening goes much further downhill."

Blake flashed her a quick, bright grin. "That's the spirit," he murmured in his own voice.

She opened her door to toss the bit of weed out of the truck, then closed it firmly again and drew a deep breath. "Okay, Tex," she said. "What are we going to do now?"

BLAKE HAD TO ADMIRE Tara's composure. Considering everything that had gone wrong that evening, it was a wonder she wasn't a basket case.

All he'd wanted was an excuse to spend time with the most appealing lawyer he'd ever met—one who had hardly given him the time of day while she worked for Carpathy, Dillon and Delacroix. He'd certainly never anticipated getting her involved in a murder case, or sending her on the run from people who seemed intent on putting a bullet in her.

Events had been spinning out of Blake's control ever since he'd seen Tara struggling with that ape in the art gallery office—or maybe when he'd waited for a contact who'd never shown up. Or even sooner, when Tara had opened her door to him, looking more lost and wounded and vulnerable than he'd ever imagined the cool, competent, almost intimidatingly intelligent attorney could appear.

Blake wasn't accustomed to being caught so completely off guard. Nor had he ever before been so distracted by a woman that he forgot to listen to his usually reliable instincts.

He was making mistakes tonight. And he hated admitting that his feelings toward Tara McBride were making him careless. He'd always been damned careful not to let anyone get in the way of his job.

He should have just asked Tara to a movie.

It was after midnight now. She looked tired when he glanced sideways at her as he pulled into the parking lot of yet another motel, this one a budget-priced, no-frills chain.

"Wait out here for a minute, okay?" he asked. "I'll get us a room."

"Blake, shouldn't we go to the police?" she asked, looking at him with searching eyes. "We have to tell them what we saw. We'll make them believe us some-how."

He understood her fear, and her automatic assumption that the police would take care of everything for them. But he didn't share her optimism. He'd been taking care of himself for too long to turn his fate over to anyone else.

"Just let me make a couple of calls first. I want to ask a few more questions, okay?"

She hesitated.

"We're both tired," he added logically. "It can't hurt to get a couple of hours' rest before we try to deal with the cops, can it?"

"Not unless they charge us with obstructing justice because we waited so long."

"Tara, we've no proof of anything we tell them. All we have is a wild tale of seeing a body in a back room, of being shot at and tracked to a motel. The police ob-viously have no body, since they're looking for a thief rather than a murderer. I've got a friend making some inquiries for me. Let me call him and find out what he's learned. Then we'll talk about what to do next."

After another long moment, Tara sighed and nod-ded. "All right. Whatever you think best."

He wanted to kiss her again. He tried to tell himself it was only because he was grateful for her trust and her courage...but since he'd wanted to kiss her from the moment he'd met her, he knew there was much more to it than that. Just as he knew this wasn't the time to follow through on the impulse.

"I'll get us a room," he repeated gruffly. "I won't take long."

He heard the truck doors lock almost as soon as he climbed out.

Tara wasn't taking the evening's adventure quite as calmly as she pretended.

THE MOTEL ROOM was even smaller than the little cabin in Marietta. It was furnished with two double beds that almost filled the room, with a nightstand between them, and a long, cheap dresser bolted to the opposite wall. There wasn't even space for a table or chairs. An open dressing area with a single sink and a bar for hanging clothes took up the back of the room and led into the tiny cubicle that held a bathtub and toilet.

"Not exactly the Ritz, is it?" Blake asked, looking around the room with a grimace. "But it's quiet, anonymous and close to the freeway in case we need to make a quick exit."

"It's clean," Tara said wearily, sitting on the edge of one of the beds. "That'll do."

Blake eyed her a bit too perceptively. "When's the last time you had a full night's sleep?"

She didn't exactly remember. She'd been so stressed over the situation at the law firm....

"I'm all right," she said.

"You're dead on your feet," Blake returned flatly. "Lie down. Get some rest. I'll make my calls and then I'll let you know when it's time to move on."

She couldn't imagine getting any sleep with him moving around the room, talking on the telephone. Watching her.

But she *was* tired. So tired that she suddenly ached.

"Maybe I'll just put my feet up for a little while," she murmured, slipping out of her shoes. Her cramped toes seemed to sigh in relief.

His thumbs hooked through the belt loops of his comfortable-looking jeans, Blake eyed her with a frown. "You can't relax in that suit. Why don't you take off the jacket and skirt?"

She thought of the scanty black bra and bikini panties she wore beneath the suit. No way was she stripping down to her underwear in front of Blake. "I'm fine," she assured him.

He reached for his bag. "Maybe there's something in here you can wear."

"Really, Blake, that's not..."

He pulled out a black fleece sweat suit and a pair of white tube socks. "This should work," he said in satisfaction. "The pants have a drawstring."

Tara looked questioningly at the duffel bag. "Just what else do you have in there?"

He grinned. "The suit, shirt and tie I was wearing earlier, the shoes I wore with it, a couple of pairs of clean underwear, one more clean shirt, and some toiletries. It really isn't a bottomless bag."

She smiled faintly in return. "I was beginning to wonder what you'd pull out next."

He lifted an eyebrow. Noting the glint in his bright blue eyes, Tara braced herself for a double-entendre reply, but Blake only tossed her the sweat suit. "You can change in the bathroom. I'll call my friend."

Tara nearly choked when she saw her reflection in the full-length mirror attached to the back of the bathroom door. Her hair was coming down in straggly wisps. Her formerly crisp dinner suit was wrinkled and there were bits of weeds and grass clinging to her skirt. Patches of bare leg showed through the rips and tears in her black panty hose.

Even her face looked different, pale and taut with violet smudges beneath her eyes. No wonder Blake had accused her of being dead on her feet. She looked like a zombie.

She took off her pearl necklace and tucked it into the right pocket of her jacket. And then she swiftly stripped off the dinner suit, tossed the shredded panty hose in the wastebasket, and donned Blake's black sweat suit and white socks. Her thoughts strayed to the image of Blake wearing the same clothes and she blushed. But she had to admit that they were much more comfortable than her own, at least for now.

The garments were too big for her, of course, but the tight bands at the wrists and ankles took up the excess length and the drawstring kept the pants from falling down. Hardly a seductive outfit, she thought critically...but then, she wasn't planning to seduce Blake, she corrected herself hastily.

The thought had never even crossed her mind.

Liar, a voice inside her head taunted. She ignored it.

Leaving her hair loose to her shoulders, and combing it with her fingers for lack of anything better to use, she opened the bathroom door and stepped out, her jacket and skirt folded over her arm.

Blake hung up the telephone just as she walked into the bedroom. He looked at her with a slight smile. "You look much more comfortable."

Feeling a bit self-conscious, she nodded and tucked a strand of hair behind her ear. "Yes, I am, thank you. Did you reach your friend?"

Something shifted in Blake's expression. "Why don't you lie down and get some rest," he said, reaching out to pull down the spread on one of the beds. "We'll talk later."

Tara narrowed her eyes, staring at him intently. "What aren't you telling me?"

"Nothing important."

But he didn't meet her eyes when he answered. Tara didn't believe him. "You said you wouldn't keep anything from me," she reminded him sternly.

He sighed and looked at her. "Even if it's something you really don't want to hear?"

"Especially then," she answered, and braced herself. "What is it?"

"My friend told me that a black sports car has been found abandoned at a motel in Marietta."

"Yours?"

He nodded. "He said that the police are looking for the owner of the vehicle—a man who was registered at the motel as Bradley Hunter—for questioning in the art gallery robbery."

"Is the car registered in your real name?"

He shook his head. "I have it on loan from a rental

company in Atlanta. Bradley Hunter was the name I used when I rented it."

"Do you *ever* use your own name?" she asked in exasperation.

"Not very often."

She was too tired to pursue that particular oddity, considering what he'd already told her. "So, someone is trying to set you up as a robbery suspect. Maybe even a murder suspect."

"It appears so."

"Why?"

"Good question. I wish I had the answer."

"Why hasn't my name gotten out? We know they have it."

"We know *someone* has it," Blake corrected her. "We don't know that the police do."

She ran a weary hand through her hair, trying to find some logic in a situation that seemed to make no sense at all. "But why? If someone is trying to set us up, wouldn't they want the police looking specifically for me?"

Blake reached down to lift her feet gently onto the bed. It was an indication of how tired she was that she didn't resist when he eased her down against the pillows, much as he would a sleepy child. "We can talk after you rest," he said, sitting on the edge of the mattress beside her.

"You haven't answered my questions," she reminded him, settling more comfortably into the pillows.

"I don't know why your name hasn't been released," he answered. "Unless whoever is after us thinks you know something that may be helpful to them if they get to us before the police do. Or something that may be harmful to them if the police find us first."

Tara raised an eyebrow. "But I don't know anything," she protested. "I'm the innocent bystander in this mess."

"Believe me, I'm aware of that," Blake said regretfully.

Tara closed her eyes—only for a moment, she promised herself. "We have to figure out what's going on," she murmured. "We have to do something."

"We will," Blake assured her. He leaned over her, bracing his left arm on the other side of her, and gently stroked a strand of hair away from her cheek with his right hand. He lingered, slowly tracing the line of her jaw with his fingertips.

Tara's eyes flew open as she became suddenly aware that she was practically lying in Blake's arms.

His face was very close to hers, his eyes focused on her mouth. He was looking at her the way he sometimes did in her fleeting daydreams. As if she was a woman a man like him could find interesting. Exciting. Desirable.

She found him all those things, of course. And more. He was everything she'd never been.

For just a moment, she had a crazy, reckless urge to reach up, wrap her arms around his neck and pull him down to her. To redirect all the pent-up energy that still lingered from their harrowing evening. But years of scrupulously developed self-control overcame that imprudent impulse. She lay still, looking up at him, wishing things were different. Wishing *she* was different.

After a moment, Blake drew back with what might have been reluctance. "Just get some rest, Tara. I'll keep watch for now."

It occurred to her that it had been a very long time since anyone had "kept watch" over her. She'd become accustomed to taking care of herself, to being totally on her own. Everyone she knew seemed to think she was too strong and tough and competent ever to depend on anyone else. It was an image she'd fostered, but one that had felt like a trap during the past two weeks.

It felt rather nice to have someone else take charge for a little while, she mused, her thoughts beginning to drift. To have someone else do the worrying and the planning for a change.

There weren't many people she would have trusted enough to put herself into their hands.

Oddly enough, considering that she hardly knew him, she trusted Blake.

It was the last clear thought she had before she allowed herself to fall asleep.

IN TARA'S DREAM, the man was lying on the floor, bleeding, his eyes open and staring into hers. Silently, he begged her to save him.

She turned to run for help, only to find herself facing the senior partners of the Carpathy, Dillon and Delacroix law firm.

"Don't just stand there gawking, Ms. McBride," Mason Carpathy ordered her sternly, glaring over the rims of his ever-present half glasses. "Take care of this situation."

"But I don't know how. I'm a lawyer, not a doctor."

"A lawyer?" Carpathy looked at his colleagues, who all smirked. "Not a very good one. We fired you, remember?"

She shook her head. "But I—"

The man on the floor moaned, reaching out to her.

"Aren't you going to help him, Ms. McBride?" Earnest Dillon demanded.

She turned to Lester Delacroix, the one partner who'd tried to defend her during her downfall, though even he had been forced to concede in the end that the longtime client who wanted her fired was more important than one young attorney. "Please, Mr. Delacroix. Help me."

He regarded her with a mixture of sympathy and disappointment. "You wouldn't listen to my advice before, Ms. McBride. Had you done so, you would still be employed. Why would you ask for my help now?"

"But this is different! Please, don't make me—"

The man on the floor gasped, coughed. His eyes rolled back.

Carpathy scowled over his glasses. "You've let him die, Ms. McBride."

"No, I—"

The other partners clucked and shook their heads. "Can't you do *anything* right, Ms. McBride?" Dillon asked critically.

"But this wasn't my fault," she protested, feeling the tears streaming down her face. "Please, I don't know—"

"You really are a failure, aren't you, Ms. McBride?" Delacroix asked sadly.

Tara looked from the disgusted partners to the dead man on the floor. "But it wasn't my fault," she whispered, feeling so desperately alone. So terribly afraid. "I tried my best."

"Failure." The word reverberated around her. "You're a failure, Tara McBride."

Failure.

4

"TARA. Tara, sweetheart, wake up."

Tara's frown deepened as Blake's voice invaded her dreams, but she didn't immediately awaken. She murmured something else he couldn't quite understand, sounding so distressed he wanted only to hold her and make the pain go away.

He touched her face, his hand not as steady as he would have liked. "Tara. Come on, honey, open your eyes."

She opened her eyes, saw Blake leaning over her, and frowned. "Did you just call me honey?" she asked, her voice still hoarse from sleep.

His mouth tilted into a smile. "You were having a bad dream."

She winced. "Did I say anything?" she asked, looking prepared to be mortified.

"Nothing coherent," he assured her. "You just seemed restless."

She ran a hand through her tousled hair and made a serious effort to wake up. "What time is it?"

He glanced at his watch. "Almost five."

"Have you had any sleep?"

"Enough." He studied her face, noting the lingering signs of strain. "Are you all right?"

She didn't meet his eyes. "Yes, I'm fine. It was just a stupid dream."

"Certainly understandable, after everything that has happened tonight. Would you like to talk about it?"

"No." She answered a bit too quickly.

He nodded. "Fine."

"I told you, it was stupid."

"It's okay, Tara. You don't have to tell me if you'd rather not."

She struggled to sit upright. Blake gave her a hand, scooting over to give her room to sit on the edge of the bed beside him.

"Have you come up with any theories about why this is happening to us?" she asked, her tone more brusque now. He could almost see her concealing her insecurities behind that tough-lawyer mask she'd perfected.

"Actually, I've been sitting here sort of recapping the evening," he admitted. "From the beginning."

"Sounds like a good idea. Maybe you could recap your recap for me."

He hadn't released her hand after helping her sit upright. He found himself unwilling to do so now. He laced his fingers with hers, letting their linked hands rest on the bed between them. And then he tried to concentrate on their conversation, rather than the feel of her soft palm pressed against his roughened one.

"Okay," he said briskly. "We went to the art gallery following a call I received from someone who knew the names of my usual contacts at the insurance company, as well as the procedures the company usually follows to contact me."

"Blake, have you ever considered getting counseling for this James Bond complex?" Tara asked with a dryness that amused him.

The corner of his mouth tilted up in a half grin. "I have to entertain myself somehow."

She frowned at him, though he thought he saw an answering smile in her eyes. "Go on."

"Right." His cleared his throat and went on. "We arrived at the art gallery and we were approached at the McCauley painting by a man in a bad toupee, who seemed to be watching us very closely."

He had suspected then that Botkin was the one who'd asked for the meeting, but he'd honestly had no sense that the man was in danger. Nor that Tara would be drawn into it, either, he thought grimly.

"At the time I'd been given," he continued, "I waited in the men's room for someone who never showed up. After a few minutes, I checked the hallway, then stepped into the main showroom to look around. When I came back, there was still no one in the hallway, but I heard a noise from the open door at the end of the hall. I had just looked into that office before I went into the showroom," he added. "No one was in there then."

"Which meant," Tara mused, "that the man in the toupee appeared right after you left. And that the other man, the one who shot him and grabbed me, was right behind him."

Blake nodded grimly. "I should have waited," he muttered, disgusted with himself. "I should never have allowed myself to be distracted by—"

You. He bit off the rest of the sentence, making Tara look at him questioningly.

"Anyway, I shouldn't have been so impatient to leave the gallery," he substituted.

"Everyone makes mistakes, Blake," Tara reassured him.

"That's something you should keep in mind, as well," he murmured. "But at least the mistake you made at the law firm—if, in fact, you made a mistake at all—didn't get anyone killed."

"And if you had waited in that hallway as you were supposed to, *you* might have been the one killed," Tara reminded him. "It's obvious that someone didn't want you to have whatever information the man was going to give you."

Blake rubbed his slightly bristly chin with his free hand. "All I was told was that it had something to do with the Willfort robbery."

"And it was so important that Botkin was killed before he could give it to you."

"That's only a guess," he cautioned her. "For all we know, he was killed by a jealous husband. Or someone who actually was trying to rob the gallery. It might only have been coincidence that you and I were there."

"Do you believe that?"

He hesitated only a fraction of a second before shaking his head. "No. I'm not a big believer in coincidence."

"Neither am I. So, apparently, I walked in just after the man was shot. The killer—whoever he was— grabbed me. He asked what the hell I was doing there." Tara shivered a bit, obviously replaying the moment in her head.

Blake's hand tightened comfortingly around hers.

"And then he asked what Botkin told me when I was kneeling down beside him. Not that I could have answered if I'd wanted to. The guy had his hand over my mouth."

Blake's hand jerked around hers. He twisted on the bed to look at her with a frown. "When you knelt beside him? But I thought you were grabbed the moment you walked into the office."

She shook her head. "I didn't see the other man at first. Maybe he hid when he heard me in the hallway."

"Tell me everything that happened in that office."

Tara didn't look as though she wanted to relive those terrifying moments, but she nodded. "I saw the man on the floor. I knelt beside him. And then he said...he said..."

"What?" Blake asked urgently.

"'They knew,'" she recalled slowly. "'The paintings were...'"

Blake frowned. "The paintings were what?"

"I don't know. That's all he said, at least I think those were his words. It was difficult to understand him."

"Nothing else?"

She shook her head. "That was it. The next thing I knew, I was being grabbed from behind. I got one good look at the man who grabbed me, the one who must have shot Botkin, but I didn't say anything to him. He didn't give me a chance. And then you came in."

"'They knew,'" Blake repeated in a murmur. "Who knew what? And the paintings he mentioned—was he talking about the paintings that were stolen from Jackson Willfort's apartment? The ones scheduled to be put on display?"

Since Tara had no answers for him, she remained silent.

Blake stared thoughtfully at the wall in front of him, musing aloud. "Willfort originally purchased the stolen paintings from the Pryce Gallery. He buys most of the art for his private collection from Liz Pryce."

"Liz Pryce?"

"Hmm. Liz Pryce owns the Pryce Gallery. She's the wife of Avery Pryce."

"Avery Pryce, the attorney?"

Blake nodded. "Right. *The* Avery Pryce, Atlanta's premier barrister. He's years older than his third wife. They've been married almost ten years. He set her up in the gallery almost immediately after they married. With his money and influence, she's been very successful. Jackson Willfort is one of her most loyal patrons, which has gone a long way toward establishing her with the rest of the art-buying community."

"How do you *know* all of this?"

He shrugged. "Someone called and said they had information about the Willfort burglary. I made a point to find out everything I could about the players before I got involved."

"So Jackson Willfort bought a couple of paintings from the Pryce Gallery that he intended to put on public display. The paintings were stolen. Someone from the gallery knew something about that robbery that he intended to share with you, but, presumably, he was murdered first. What could he have known? Who is now in possession of my name and address, and what do they think I know that could be dangerous to them?"

"I don't know what Botkin was trying to tell you, but we're going to try to find out. Our 'friends' are now after you because they think he told you too much. And they don't want you telling anyone. As for me—they aren't sure who I am or how much I know, but they're probably hoping the cops will lead them to me, and then they'll be able to take care of both of us at once."

"Do you think they're still in my apartment?"

That seemed to bother Tara almost as much as everything else. He wrapped her hand in both of his. "I don't know," he said gently. "But we can assume it isn't safe for us to go there for now."

She took a deep breath and again spoke firmly. "So what do we do now?"

He smiled and lifted her hand to his lips, brushing a kiss across her knuckles. "Looks like we're about to be partners in an investigation, Tara McBride," he said in the Texas drawl he sometimes affected. "Think you can handle it?"

SHE COULD handle it, Tara told herself dazedly. She could deal with the knowledge that someone wanted to find her—for deadly reasons she didn't understand.

But she wasn't at all sure she could handle Blake. Not if he kept smiling at her that way. Holding her hand. Kissing her.

In his own way, Blake was as dangerous to her peace of mind as the man who might even now be pawing through her things in the apartment.

"You didn't get much sleep," Blake said, finally releasing her hand. "Would you like to crash for a while longer?"

Feeling oddly bereft without the comfort of his touch, she ran her hand through her hair and shook her head. "I couldn't sleep now. What I'd really like is a shower."

He nodded, then frowned. "You don't have any clean clothes to put on."

"I don't have anything," she said simply. "Shampoo, hairbrush, toothbrush, underwear."

Blake stood. "Okay," he said, reaching for his duffel bag. He tossed her a plastic bottle and a man's denim shirt. "Here's some shampoo. You take a shower and use that shirt for a bathrobe. I'll go out and find a twenty-four-hour discount store, pick up a few basic supplies, as well as a change of clothes and a pair of sneakers for you. What are your sizes?"

Surely he wasn't thinking of buying her underwear, she thought, biting her lips as she stared at him.

"Tara," Blake said patiently, "we're in a difficult situation here. We're going to have to be practical. Until we get this resolved, we'll be spending a lot of time together. It's the only way I can protect you. You've trusted me this far. Don't stop now."

Annoyed with herself for acting like a schoolgirl, Tara nodded. "I do trust you. I'm sorry, I just don't quite know what to do. I'm completely out of my element."

"Believe me, sweetheart, I know the feeling." There was an ironic twist to his words that she didn't quite understand. "What are your sizes?"

She reached for the pad and pen that sat on the nightstand. Without hesitating again, she scribbled sizes—bra, panties, shirt, jeans, shoes. She then ripped the sheet off and handed it to him.

Blake turned and headed for the door. "I won't be long," he said. "Put the chain on behind me and don't open this door for anyone but me."

She nodded. "Be careful, Blake."

The grin he shot her could only be described as cocky. "Worried about me, are you?"

"No. I just really need a toothbrush."

"Any color preference?"

"Pink," she shot back without hesitation.

He wrinkled his nose. "You're going to make me go out there and buy a pink toothbrush?"

She smiled. He hadn't blinked at buying lingerie, but he complained about the pink toothbrush. "Don't come back without it," she ordered imperiously.

He laughed and let himself out. Then tapped on the door. "Chain," he said quietly through the wood.

She didn't hear him walk away until she'd secured the locks and the chain. Moments later, she heard the muted roar of his truck engine as he drove away from the motel in the early-morning silence.

But he would be back, she thought, and all her nerve endings seemed to tingle in anticipation.

JUGGLING BAGS, Blake tapped on the motel-room door a little over half an hour later. "It's me," he said, hearing Tara on the other side. "And I have your pink tooth-brush," he added, just in case she had any doubt of his identity.

The door opened. She stood there with wet hair and clean-scrubbed face, wearing his oversize denim shirt, which covered her to her knees. Beneath the shirt, her legs and feet were bare.

And, despite his promise that she could trust him, and his own private vow that he would not take advantage of her temporary dependence on him, Blake was hit with a wave of hunger so intense that he had to clear his throat. He'd wanted Tara McBride since the first time he'd seen her. He wanted her even more now.

He told himself not to even *think* along those lines until he'd gotten her out of the mess he'd dragged her into. But, damn, she looked good fresh out of the shower, wearing nothing but his shirt.

Her expression self-conscious, she stood back and let him enter, then closed and locked the door behind her. Trying to put her at ease, Blake hid his reaction to her and tossed all but one bag on the bed she'd slept in.

"The selection was rather limited, but this stuff should do for now. I've brought breakfast, too," he added, tapping the fast-food bag in his hand. "I'll set it out while you get dressed."

Tara dug into the well-stuffed blue plastic bags on the bed, pulling out jeans and two T-shirts—one aqua-and-white striped, the other white with red piping—a package of white sport socks, white canvas sneakers, a deodorant stick "for ladies only," a travel-size hairdryer, and a hairbrush. Blake had bought everything he could think of that a woman might need when she was stranded with nothing.

She blushed rosily when she found the undergarments he'd selected—white lace bikini panties and a lacy white bra.

He liked it when she blushed. He got the feeling it wasn't something she did very often.

And then she found the things in the bottom of the bag. A powder compact. Blush, mascara and lipstick. He'd had to ask for help with those selections, but it was worth it, judging by Tara's reaction. Blake's sister had once told him that a woman couldn't help but feel better about herself if she was wearing a little makeup.

Blake had hoped Tara would like the stuff, but he hadn't expected her to look up at him with tears in her beautiful sky-blue eyes.

"I—er—know it's not the good stuff you probably buy at Saks or Neiman's, but it's the best I could find at this hour."

"Blake, thank you."

The tears, the slight tremor in her lower lip, the little break in her voice shook him. "Tara, it's only makeup."

She gave him an unsteady smile and made a quick swipe at her cheek. "I know. I guess I'm still a little tired."

"You need food," he said awkwardly, willing to do just about anything to dry those tears. "I brought muffins. I hope you like blueberry."

Her smile deepened. "I love blueberry."

Relieved that she seemed to have her emotions under control again, he nodded. "There are two foam cups of coffee getting cold in the bottom of the bag. You might want to hurry and get dressed."

She gathered her new clothes into her arms. "I'll just be a minute," she promised.

She paused as she passed him on the way to the bathroom. After only a momentary hesitation, she rose on tiptoe and pressed a quick kiss to his unshaven cheek. "It was a very sweet gesture, Blake," she murmured, drawing away. "Thank you."

Without even stopping to think about it, he snagged a hand behind her wet head, pulled her toward him and planted a long, firm kiss against her mouth. This was the third time he'd kissed her, and each time she tasted sweeter, more inviting. If he wasn't careful, if he kept indulging in those addictive kisses, he was going to do something monumentally stupid.

Blake's pulse was racing when he pulled away, and Tara's eyes were huge. He took a quick step back, out of the danger zone.

"You're welcome," he said, his voice husky. "Now go get dressed before I forget all those promises about how trustworthy I am."

She wasted no time closing herself into the bathroom.

Blake ran an unsteady hand through his hair and wasted a few minutes calling himself every synonym he could think of for fool. And then he turned to set out blueberry muffins and rapidly cooling coffee.

They had a long day ahead of them, with no time for distractions. Once he'd figured out what the hell was going on, and had got everything under control...well, then he would see whether Tara McBride still considered him "sweet."

TARA AVOIDED Blake's eyes while they ate their hasty breakfast. He probably thought she was an idiot. She couldn't believe she'd made such a fuss over a few inexpensive cosmetics. She wasn't one to burst into tears that way. She must have been more tired than she'd thought.

As for that kiss...well, she simply couldn't think about that right now.

After they'd eaten, Blake took a shower while Tara dried her hair and applied a touch of the makeup. She told herself it was merely a measure of her stress and exhaustion that she almost sniffled again when she opened her bright pink toothbrush.

She tried to block out the sound of the water running in the shower. Tried to push away the mental images of Blake standing naked beneath it. But it was impossible to forget the feeling of his mouth pressed hard to hers.

Don't do this, Tara.

She was in no position to get involved with anyone, much less an enigmatic, unpredictable, adventure-seeking private investigator. Even before she'd lost her job, when she'd seen Blake occasionally and had felt the tug of attraction every time, she'd known it was foolish. A dashing P.I., she'd told herself, couldn't possibly be interested in a serious, routine-bound tax attorney.

She had never learned to flirt, something Blake did with a skill and enthusiasm that indicated years of successful practice. Tara hadn't even had a steady boyfriend in high school. Her cousin Savannah, who'd been the captain of the cheerleader squad and extremely popular with the boys, had accused Tara of intimidating the guys with her brains and ambition.

Not that flirting had paid off for Savannah, who'd ended up pregnant and ignominiously dumped by her boyfriend at seventeen. Witnessing her cousin's humiliation, Tara had told herself that she wasn't interested in dating—and then had tried to believe it.

College had been a blur of studying and exams. Tara had finished in three years and had then been accepted into Harvard Law School. After that had come the offer from the law firm in Atlanta.

She'd dated now and then, of course. She'd even tried to have a meaningful relationship with a suitable young attorney whose ambition matched her own—a bit too closely, actually, since it had been his jealousy over her success that had driven them apart.

But no way was she prepared to indulge in a fling with Blake. As far as she could see, nothing could come of it but a broken heart and another devastating blow to her already battered ego. Maybe if she *had* learned to flirt somewhere along the way…if she could trust herself to enjoy Blake's attentions without reading too much into them, or wanting too much from him…

If only she was as reckless and adventurous as Blake… But she wasn't.

So, no more kissing Blake, no matter how sweet he was, she told herself sternly. From now on, she was keeping her lips strictly to herself.

Lacking a case, she scooped the cosmetics into the same blue plastic bag Blake had brought them in. She wondered if she should wash her worn lingerie out by hand and let it dry over the shower rod. She didn't know how long Blake intended to remain in this room. Not long, she hoped. The walls were already beginning to close in on her.

She heard the bathroom door open, and automatically glanced around. Blake emerged wearing a pair of jeans and the denim shirt she'd had on earlier. His hair was wet, and he hadn't yet buttoned the shirt. It hung loose over his jeans, revealing a sleek, firm chest glistening with a sheen of moisture. And Tara felt her knees start to melt.

There were parts of her, she thought in despair, that hadn't yet gotten the message that this man was out of her league.

"I've been thinking," he said, apparently oblivious to her stunned reaction to his appearance. "The stolen paintings may be the key to finding out what's going on. If we can find them, maybe we can find our answers."

Tara cleared her throat. "And how would you suggest we go about that?"

"I have this friend..." He rubbed his clean-shaven chin and frowned, looking thoughtfully at Tara. "Maybe you'd better stay here. You'll be safe here."

No way was she staying in this claustrophobic little room while Blake went off looking for clues. She shook her head. "No."

"Tara..."

"No, Blake. I'd go crazy sitting here alone, wondering where you were and when you'd be back. Wondering if the next knock on the door would be you...or a man with a gun. Wherever you're going, I want to go with you."

He sighed. "I can't blame you, really. I wouldn't want to be left behind, either."

Relieved, she nodded. "So, what next?"

He glanced at his watch. "It's still early. Maybe we can catch the Spider before he gets busy."

"The...Spider?" she repeated, hoping she hadn't heard him correctly.

He gave her a wry smile. "That's what they call him."

"And what's his real name?"

"I'm not sure anyone knows that...including him."

"Oh." She swallowed, then firmed her chin. "All right. Let's go find this Spider person."

He chuckled. "Let me finish getting dressed. Spider's pad is one place I definitely wouldn't want to go into barefoot."

She pictured a dark, deadly web and almost shuddered, then chided herself for letting her imagination get away from her. She sat on the end of her bed and watched from the corner of her eye while Blake dried his hair, brushed his teeth, buttoned and tucked in his shirt. It was a small room, she reminded herself. She had no choice but to watch him.

He sat on the edge of his own bed, and opened the drawer to the tiny nightstand. He pulled out an odd-looking leather sheath with straps. And then he rolled up the right leg of his jeans.

Tara watched in open curiosity as Blake strapped the thin leather sheath to his leg. "Is that a...knife?" she asked, staring at the black handle nestled into the holder.

Without immediately answering, Blake pulled on

his boots, making sure the knife handle was still accessible above the right one, then smoothed his loose, straight-cut jeans down over them, completely concealing the sheath. And then he looked at Tara.

"It never hurts to be prepared," he said, confirming her guess.

Tara had to remind herself that she'd insisted he take her along.

Blake carefully gathered every article they'd brought into the motel with them and shoved them into the duffel bag. Everything that didn't fit went into the plastic bags he'd carried in earlier. By the time he'd loaded everything into the truck, there was no evidence that they'd been there except for the trash in the wastebaskets.

"We won't be coming back here?" Tara asked.

He shook his head. "No. Even if we have to spend another night in a motel, I'd rather be in a different one."

She glanced somewhat wistfully around the tiny room as she followed Blake out. Maybe it had been small and dingy, but it had been safe. And all of a sudden, she wasn't in such a hurry to leave.

5

THE ATLANTA NEIGHBORHOOD Blake drove through was one that Tara usually avoided. Crumbling, abandoned buildings and trash-filled empty lots surrounded them. It was still early enough that there was little traffic on the streets, and few people on the broken sidewalks. The heavily clouded skies overhead emphasized the grim hopelessness of the area.

Blake drove the truck into a particularly dark, ugly alley, and parked in front of a couple of broken, rusted Dumpsters. He nodded toward a metal door almost hidden in the shadows. The building appeared to be an abandoned warehouse. "Spider's usually in there this early in the day."

"This is where he lives?" Tara's voice sounded a bit shaky even to her own ears.

"On and off. You coming in with me or waiting out here?"

She reached immediately for the door handle. "I'm staying close to you."

He flashed her a quick grin. "I like the sound of that."

She gave him a chiding look—how could he be flirting when their lives were on the line? But she still couldn't help smiling back at him.

Blake paused with one hand on the door latch. "I'd, er, better warn you that Spider's a bit...well, odd."

She rolled her eyes. "Trust me, that possibility had already crossed my mind."

To Tara's surprise, the heavy metal door wasn't locked. It opened with a shiver-inducing shriek from its rusted hinges. Whoever was inside had to have heard their arrival.

Tara didn't know if that was good or bad.

Blake took Tara's hand as he led her into the building. He did that a lot, she mused. He was obviously a toucher. She never had been, herself. But that was beginning to change.

Inside, the old building smelled of dirt, mold, decay...and a few other odors Tara didn't want to try to identify. It seemed to be empty, except for piles of refuse and abandoned parts to old warehouse equipment. What little light there was came from high, metal-mesh-reinforced windows. Even if the sun had been shining brightly outside, the filthy glass wouldn't have let in much light. As it was, there was hardly enough illumination for them to pick their way carefully through the maze of junk toward the even more deeply shadowed back of the building.

Tara heard something rustle in a corner, followed by what sounded like an animal squeaking. She lifted her chin and hid her fear, determined that she could act as casual about this as Blake.

A gruff voice spoke suddenly from the shadows. "Hey, Blake."

Blake stopped. Tara looked cautiously around, but couldn't see the man who'd spoken.

"Hey, Spider," Blake answered casually. "How's it going?"

"Can't complain. You?"

"Oh, the usual. Someone's trying to kill me. I think I'm being framed for a murder. You know...same old grind."

Spider gave a raspy chuckle. "You really need to get a job with a bit more excitement in it."

"Yeah, I was thinking of taking up accounting."

"Like anybody would trust you with their money. What's that you're wearing on your arm?"

Tara glanced automatically at Blake's arms, wondering what in the world the guy meant.

"This is my friend, Tara," Blake answered, and Tara frowned in sudden comprehension. "Tara, say hi to Spider."

"Hello, Spider," she said a bit coolly.

"Nice to meetcha, ma'am. You a spook, too?"

"Tara's not a P.I. She's a lawyer," Blake answered for her.

"Oh. A lawyer."

The tone of revulsion in which the man repeated her profession made Tara's frown deepen.

What might have been a faint ripple of amusement lay beneath Blake's voice when he spoke again. "She just got fired."

"You don't say." Spider suddenly sounded more approving. "Well, what brings y'all to my humble abode?"

"The Willfort robbery."

"What about it?"

"I'm looking for the paintings," Blake answered

lightly. "Don't care about the rest of the stuff, just the art."

"Can't help you." Spider's rejection sounded friendly enough, but firm.

Tara looked inquiringly at Blake.

"Can't or won't?" Blake asked.

"Can't, Bubba. Ain't no one knows where they are. At least, not so's I've heard."

Now it was Blake who frowned. "You haven't even heard a rumor?"

"You doubtin' my word, Blake?" The voice had gone very quiet.

Blake sighed loudly. "You know better than that, Spider. I'm just frustrated, that's all."

"Yeah, well..." The other man grudgingly accepted the implied apology.

"If you ask me," Spider said after a moment, "there's somethin' fishy about that whole thing."

"I'm asking you," Blake said.

"No one's talking about it. Matter of fact, everyone seems to be real careful *not* to talk about it, if you know what I mean. This ain't no ordinary, everyday B and E."

"So you don't think it's local?"

"Hell, I'm sure it ain't. If anybody would know, it'd be me."

Blake pulled something out of his jeans pocket, and laid it on top of a broken crate. "I appreciate this, Spider."

"Hey, that's what friends are for, man," the disembodied voice drawled. "You take care, ma'am. Don't let this rascal get you into more trouble than you can handle, you hear?"

Tara didn't quite know how to answer that, since in her mind, it was already too late. She said only, "Goodbye, Spider."

Blake turned and led Tara out of the building without another word.

THOUGH IT WASN'T significantly brighter outside, considering the heavy cloud cover overhead, it felt almost like stepping out of the night and into the day. The odors of the alley weren't notably sweeter than those inside the old warehouse, but it was still fresh air. Blake inhaled gratefully, wondering how Spider could stand to spend so much time in that tomblike environment.

He released Tara's hand so that he could open the driver's door to the truck and let her slide in. Surreptitiously, he flexed his fingers, which had gone rather numb. He'd been impressed by how well she'd handled the admittedly strange encounter with Spider, but the way she'd gripped Blake's hand had hinted that she wasn't quite as calm as she'd acted.

"Are you okay?" he asked, turning to her as he got in behind the wheel and closed the door.

"Yes, I'm fine, thank you," she answered with almost humorous politeness.

"You weren't frightened in there, were you?" he asked, his hand still tingling as the circulation returned slowly to his fingertips.

"No, of course not," she replied, daring him to doubt her.

He couldn't help himself. He leaned across the seat and settled his lips warmly, firmly on hers. And, after only a momentary hesitation, she responded.

By the time he drew back, she had lost that slightly stunned look she'd worn since they'd left the warehouse. She blinked as though just waking up from a bizarre dream—which only made him want to kiss her again. So he did.

"I really have to stop doing this," he murmured against her lips.

"Yes. You really do." Her voice was husky.

Reluctantly, he straightened, started the engine and backed carefully out of the alley.

His meeting with Spider hadn't been as productive as Blake had hoped, but it had certainly given him some things to think about.

THE RAIN STARTED almost as soon as they were back in the truck. Torrents of it slashed across the windshield, accompanied by rumbling thunder and buffeting wind.

"Where are we going now?" Tara asked as Blake drove onto the freeway. She'd had to raise her voice somewhat to be heard over the storm.

"Another motel, I think," he replied. "We don't want to be combing the streets for information in this weather. And I've got a couple more calls I want to make. This time, we'll find a place on the other side of Atlanta—Monroe, maybe."

She nodded. She no longer questioned Blake's cloak-and-dagger games. After meeting Spider—sort of—Tara was prepared for anything.

It was close to lunch time when they arrived in Monroe and spotted a likely-looking motel. A fast-food restaurant with a drive-through window was nearby, so Blake stopped there first, saying they would eat in their room, where they could talk in private.

Again, Tara waited in the truck while Blake rented a room. He wore his black cowboy hat again, and strolled through the rain with the same lanky-cowboy walk he'd feigned before. Tara wondered what name he'd given this time.

An odd feeling rippled through her when it occurred to her that she had just spent the night with a man whose real last name she didn't even know. She was going to have to find out more about Blake before she trusted him much further with her life, she decided with a frown.

They managed to get inside without getting thoroughly drenched. Then they sat cross-legged on separate beds to eat.

"Where did you meet that Spider guy?" Tara asked as she unwrapped her sandwich.

"Around," Blake answered vaguely, lifting a soda can to his lips. He took a drink, then asked wryly, "He's quite a character, isn't he?"

"To say the least." She shook her head, remembering the bizarre encounter. "Why didn't he want us to see him?"

Blake shrugged. "It's just a little quirk he has. He's, er, shy."

"Yeah. Right."

She ate a french fry, then said, "I have to admit, I

didn't understand half of what you guys were talking about. Did you learn anything useful from him?"

"Maybe." Blake seemed to drift into his own thoughts.

Tara cleared her throat, determined to be brought up to date. "And...?"

"What? Oh." He gave her a faintly apologetic smile. "Spider has what you might call an inside track on tracing stolen merchandise. Even if he can't lead me right to it, he can generally point me in the right direction."

"But he couldn't even do that in this case."

"Right. He hasn't heard a word, and that's odd, considering how much was taken and how much publicity the robbery got."

"He seemed to be implying that people are actually afraid to talk about the robbery."

"That's exactly what he was implying," Blake said with a nod.

"If only we knew what the man at the gallery wanted to tell you about the robbery," Tara said wistfully.

"We'll just have to find out on our own," Blake said bracingly. Then added with a bit less confidence, "Somehow."

He tossed his trash in a wastebasket and reached for the telephone.

"Who are you calling?"

"I know someone in the insurance company who might have something useful for us."

"But will you be able to reach him on a Saturday?"

"Good question." He turned his attention to the telephone.

Deciding to give him at least a semblance of privacy, Tara busied herself clearing up the rest of the trash from their lunch.

She wondered if she should call her parents after Blake finished with the phone. She didn't know what she'd tell them, but she certainly wouldn't want them calling her apartment and having a strange man answer, assuming the jerk was still haunting her home, waiting for her to return. She shuddered at the very thought.

She didn't expect them to call, since she'd led them to believe she would be out of reach for several weeks. She'd told herself she'd needed that time to pull herself together, to get on with things after the disaster at Carpathy, Dillon and Delacroix. Still, maybe it would be best to make sure.

Blake slammed the telephone down with a muttered curse. "Answering machine," he said in response to Tara's questioning look.

"I suppose you don't want to leave this number."

"That wouldn't be my first choice, no."

Tara sat on the edge of the other bed and ran a hand through her hair. "What next?" she asked wearily, feeling as if they'd been on the run for days.

Knees touching hers, Blake leaned forward and took her hands—a habit of his that she was beginning to like a little too much. "You holding up okay?"

"I'm fine," she assured him without quite meeting his eyes. "I just hope you know what you're doing by not going to the police."

"Sweetheart, I'm not sure I know what I'm doing at all," he answered wryly.

"What's the worst that could happen if we go to the police?"

"We could be jailed for theft—if not murder."

"They have no evidence."

His eyebrow rose. "They have witnesses who saw us at the gallery, talking to the man who was murdered minutes later. Who knows what other evidence has been planted against us?"

"And if we don't go to the police?"

"Then we try to find out what's going on without letting the killer find us first."

Tara supposed she should appreciate Blake's honesty. He certainly wasn't sugarcoating anything. But maybe just a little sugarcoating wouldn't hurt?

No. She wanted the truth, she decided. She was no meek victim, needing to be protected from the facts. Though neither of them had intended it to happen, she had become a partner in this investigation—and she expected to be treated like one.

"What are we going to do now?" she asked again.

A loud clap of thunder prevented him from answering immediately. The lights in the room dimmed for an instant, making Tara hope fervently that there wouldn't be a power outage.

"Maybe we should just wait out the storm for a while," Blake suggested. "I'll try at regular intervals to reach Bill—the guy from the insurance company. After that...we'll play it by ear."

They'd been doing that all along, as far as Tara could tell.

ANOTHER QUIET MOTEL room, the only sound the steady pounding of rain against the window. Another cozy area, where two beds filled up most of the space. Another stretch of time with nothing for Blake to do except watch Tara and secretly wonder what it would be like if they were to spend that time making good use of one of those beds.

Needing to burn his restless energy, he began to pace, his hands in his pockets. He wished idly that he had something to juggle.

Tara sat cross-legged on one of the beds, watching him. He could almost feel her gaze following him around the room, which seemed to get smaller each time he crossed it.

"Feeling a little claustrophobic?" she asked finally.

He stopped pacing and lifted one shoulder. "Maybe a little."

"I'd have thought a P.I. would be used to this sort of thing. Don't most stakeouts consist of long hours of boredom and inactivity?"

"Yeah," he admitted. "But at least I feel like I'm in charge when I'm on a stakeout. I know what's going on."

"How long have you been a private investigator?"

"Close to ten years now, I guess."

Tara's eyebrows lifted, as though his answer had surprised her. "How old are you?"

He didn't mind the personal question. "Thirty-four."

"Oh. I thought you were younger."

Leaning back against the dresser, with his legs

crossed in front of him, Blake chuckled. "I'll take that as a compliment."

"Still, you were very young when you got started. Was your father an investigator? A police officer, perhaps?"

Blake's quick laugh was rough-edged. "No, my father wasn't a cop. He would have been appalled at the very idea."

Blake's father hadn't had a lot of faith in cops. Or in anyone else who represented stability and authority.

"Would have been?" Tara repeated, picking up on the wording.

"He died when I was barely fifteen." Blake kept his voice light, but his smile had vanished.

"What about your mother? Is she still living?"

"They died together, in an accident." An accident Blake still felt responsible for, after all this time. An accident that still haunted him at times when he let his guard down, or on those rare occasions when he thought wistfully of someday having a home or family of his own.

"Oh, Blake, how terrible for you. You were so young to lose them both. I'm so sorry."

"It was almost twenty years ago," he reminded her, uncomfortable with her sympathy.

"But it still hurts," she said, a bit too perceptively.

He was silent for a time, then cleared his throat and answered candidly. "Yes. I still hate hospitals. My mom lived a few days after the accident, and I'll always associate the sounds and smells of hospitals with her death."

Blake shook off the painful memories. "What about

your parents?" he asked, sensing that she wanted to make conversation. Maybe she was fighting a touch of cabin fever, herself.

"Still living in Honoria, Georgia, the little town where I was born. My father's a small-town attorney, my mother's a schoolteacher. We're the respectable branch of the McBride family," she added wryly.

Respectable. A word that had never been applied to Blake's family. Which only served as another reminder of how differently he and Tara had been raised. "Is that right?"

"Oh, yes. Mom and Dad haven't caused any scandals in thirty years. My younger brothers and I were almost perfect children. I went to Harvard. Trevor works for the State Department in Washington, D.C. My youngest brother, Trent, is a senior at the Air Force Academy. All in all, we're a model of respectability, unlike the rest of the McBrides. Or at least we were—until I managed to get myself fired," she added, apparently trying without success to keep the bitterness from her voice.

Sounded as though her family could have modeled for those Rockwell paintings she'd asked about at the art gallery. Or starred in one of those TV sitcom families Blake had watched—and sometimes secretly envied—as a child.

He looked at Tara speculatively. "You haven't told your family yet about what happened at the law firm, have you?"

She looked away from him. "No."

"Why not?"

She shrugged.

"Are you afraid they won't understand? That they'll be disappointed in you?" He'd have thought a family like the one she'd described would have immediately rallied around one of their own who'd fallen on hard times. At least, that was what he'd always imagined typical families did.

She shook her head. "I know they'd understand, and they would be there for me, even if they were disappointed. I just haven't been ready to talk about it yet. To anyone."

She'd talked about it to Blake, a little, he couldn't help thinking with a touch of satisfaction. He wondered what bothered Tara more—the loss of her position, or the humiliation of feeling as if she'd failed at something. "Did you *like* your job?" he asked.

She hesitated so long that he suspected she didn't quite know the answer. "I didn't dislike it," she said finally. "It was a job, you know? I was good at it—despite the evidence to the contrary."

"I never doubted that," he assured her. "What happened?"

"I refused to sign off on something that a very important client demanded. It was a foreign tax shelter—very iffy. After researching it for months, I decided it was just too risky. I didn't want anything to do with it. The client pitched a fit, the senior partners tried to pressure me into going along, and I refused. I thought, when it came to the crunch, my associates would back me. They didn't."

He scowled. "Even if you were right?"

She shrugged. "Their risk analysis showed that their liability wouldn't be that great if everything fell apart.

The client would take the fall...and there was a slim chance that I would take it with him. The partners would quietly pocket their huge retainers and look the other way. The client would just find some other attorney to do what he wanted, they said, and they intended to make sure that didn't happen. So, they dumped me and promoted someone with a few less scruples."

"What are you going to do now?"

"I don't know. I'll hardly get a glowing recommendation from Carpathy, Dillon and Delacroix."

"You'll recover," Blake predicted confidently. "You'll go into an interview with your chin high and convince the next employer that you know what you're doing and you don't let anyone steer you wrong. What you did took guts and integrity, and you'll find someone who recognizes your strength."

She didn't look entirely convinced, but Blake had no doubt that he was right. Tara was too smart, too talented, too capable to stay down for long.

"I have no doubt that you can do anything you want to do, Tara McBride. The only question you should ask yourself is what do you really *want* to do?"

It had been so long since Tara had asked herself that question that she didn't even know how to begin to figure out the answer. All her life, it seemed, she had done what everyone else wanted her to do.

Be a good girl, Tara. Study hard, Tara. Go to Harvard, Tara. Be a lawyer, Tara.

Go away, Ms. McBride.

She thought of that childish letter she'd written to herself and buried in a makeshift time capsule. A letter filled with other people's dreams, other people's ambitions for her. And she realized she was no closer to knowing what she truly wanted now than she had been at fourteen.

Blake seemed to understand that she needed some time to think about what he'd said. So he changed the subject back to their more immediate problem. "How many people do you suppose have tried to call you at your apartment since we left yesterday?"

She bit her lip before answering. "Very few, if any," she said after a moment. "My family thinks I'm out of town. My friends think I'm in Honoria. I wasn't expecting anyone to call."

"I'd like to call your place again," Blake mused, frowning at the telephone. "Just to see who answers, if anyone. But I don't want to be traced here, the way we were in Marietta. Will your phone accept calls if I dial in anonymously?"

She shook her head, feeling as if she should apologize. "I've had all anonymous calls blocked. My number's unlisted, but I've still been careful."

"Good idea. Usually," he added with a slight smile. "So if I disconnect the caller-ID feature on this phone, I'll get what?"

"A recorded message instructing you to disconnect the privacy feature and call again."

"That option is out, then."

"Don't you have a cell phone? We couldn't be traced through that, could we?"

"Depends on who we're dealing with. But I might risk it, anyway...if I hadn't left my cell phone in the sports car in Marietta. It's probably in a police-compound lot right now. Talk about stupid mistakes..."

He shook his head in self-castigation, then glanced at his watch. Tara automatically did the same, noting that it was almost 2:00 p.m. Another clap of thunder rattled the windows, and the rain pounded the pavement outside the little room. Tara heard no other noises outside. She was suddenly very aware again of being alone with Blake inside this cozy motel room.

She cleared her throat, and slid casually to the edge of her bed, planting both feet firmly on the floor. "I wish there was something we could do to make the time pass faster," she murmured, her sudden attack of self-consciousness making her speak before thinking.

Blake immediately got that mischievous look in his eyes that she was beginning to recognize. He moved to the end of the other bed and tested the mattress with his hand. And then he looked at her in a way that set her pulse racing. "I'm sure I can come up with an idea or two," he murmured.

She could probably come up with a few, herself, for that matter. But that didn't mean she was going to follow through on them. She was already in enough trouble without tumbling into bed with Blake Whatever-his-name-was!

She gave him a repressive look. "We could watch television."

"I had something a bit more interesting in mind," he said with exaggerated regret.

She struggled against a sudden smile. Darn it, why did he have to be so gorgeous and charming. He made it really hard for her to keep her head straight where he was concerned. "Behave yourself."

Looking rather pleased with himself, Blake picked up the television remote. "I'll try," he murmured and tuned in to a soap opera, then settled back to watch it.

Tara wasn't able to lose herself in the daytime drama. She had too many problems of her own to be interested in the fictional imbroglios unfolding on the tiny screen. Not the least of them, her heart-fluttering, decidedly unwise reactions to the man sitting on the other bed.

6

TARA DIDN'T remember falling asleep. But she woke curled in the middle of the bed, only to find herself alone in the little motel room. A quick glance at her watch told her that she must have slept for a couple of hours. She parted the curtain an inch to look outside.

Even through the heavy sheets of rain, she could see that the black pickup truck was gone. Blake had left her here alone.

Tara almost gave in to a moment of sharp, instinctive panic. How could Blake have left her stranded this way?

And then her common sense slowly overcame the fear.

Blake wouldn't have left her. She didn't know where he'd gone, or when he would return...but she knew he'd come back for her. He'd asked her to trust him. Against all reason, perhaps, she trusted him with her life.

She tried to be patient until he returned. She flipped channels on the television, searching for something to catch her interest, but nothing did. She thought wistfully of the unread novel on the nightstand in her apartment. She hadn't been able to concentrate enough to enjoy reading during the past couple of weeks, but if she had it now, she could...

No, perhaps not. She wasn't sure a hair-raising murder mystery would be something she should read just now.

Her attention fell on the duffel bag sitting at the foot of one of the beds. She doubted that Blake had a book in there. But she supposed it couldn't hurt to look. She had nothing else to do. She didn't think he'd mind, since he'd already given her access to his things.

She didn't find a book. What she found, at the very bottom of the bag, was a stack of ID cards bound with a rubber band, all bearing photographs of Blake. Each card bore a different name.

It seemed somehow inevitable that he would choose that moment to return. She still had the cards in her hand when he unlocked the door and walked into the room.

"I was looking for something to read," she said inanely.

Removing his damp hat, he glanced at the ID cards, apparently unperturbed by her snooping. "Find anything interesting?"

Mimicking his insouciant tone, she shrugged and stuffed the cards back into the bag. "Not particularly."

Blake tossed his hat on the dresser and ran a hand through his hair. "I'll be glad when this rain stops," he said. "A guy could drown out there."

"Where have you been?" she asked, still trying to speak casually.

"Back to Atlanta to make some calls from a pay phone. I got the answering machine at your apartment, by the way. Either they've left the place, or they're screening calls through the machine. Either way, it would still be unwise for us to go there."

Though it had been less than twenty-four hours since she'd left her apartment, it suddenly felt like days. Tara thought wistfully of her clothes, her things, her own bed...and then she told herself to stop wishing things were different and concentrate on helping Blake.

"Did you have a good nap?" Blake asked, smiling. "You were sleeping so soundly when I left that I hated to disturb you."

"Yes, I feel much more rested, thank you. You, um, might have left me a note or something, though," she couldn't help reprimanding him. "When I woke up and couldn't find you, I wondered where you'd gone."

He frowned, looking at her questioningly. "Surely you didn't think I'd left you here?"

"The thought crossed my mind for a moment. Once I stopped to think about it, though, I knew you'd be back."

"Thank you for trusting me," he said quietly.

She shrugged, and changed the subject. "Did you find your friend from the insurance company?"

Blake's eyes turned grim, letting her know that she wasn't going to like his answer. She was struck for a moment by how quickly she was learning to read his expressions.

"I reached him," Blake said flatly.

"And?"

"He didn't know anything about what's happened to us. He claimed he had no idea I'd been asked to delve into the Willfort robbery. According to him, there had been no reason to believe it was anything other than what Willfort reported to the police. And he'd never heard the name of the so-called insurance-company employee who contacted me."

"Do you believe him? That he knew nothing about it, I mean?"

"Yeah," Blake answered reluctantly. "I believe him. Which means I've been a total idiot."

She immediately bristled on his behalf. "In what way?"

"I didn't verify," he admitted. "I always verify an assignment. This time, I just took the caller's instructions at face value and followed them without a qualm. Not only that, I pulled you into it without knowing what I was getting into. I don't know how to tell you how sorry I am about that."

"You have nothing to apologize to me for. You've already said you had no idea this case would turn dangerous when you asked me to join you."

"I just wanted an excuse to take you out," he admitted, startling her. "I thought you could be my date at the gallery, give me a little cover for being there, and then we could go out for a nice dinner afterward. I didn't expect to be at the gallery more than forty-five minutes or so—just long enough for me to meet my contact and let him slip me an envelope."

"I have to admit I was a little surprised when you showed up at my apartment," she said, feeling suddenly a bit shy. "It wasn't as if we knew each other well."

He didn't smile when he looked at her, and something in his eyes made her pulse trip. "That was always a situation I had hoped to remedy."

Tara suddenly found herself having difficulty breathing normally. Blake had been interested in her before she'd left the law firm? All those times during the past couple of years when he'd stopped by her desk with a smile and a teasing remark, she'd told herself that he did so only to be polite. That she'd been no more special to him than the other associates in the firm, all of whom he never failed to greet with equal charm.

Had he really looked at her differently?

Blake exhaled and looked away, breaking the sudden taut silence between them. "This really isn't the time to get into that," he said. "First, we have to get out of this mess I've gotten us into."

Tara tried to speak normally. "What do we do next?"

"I still think the missing art is the key," he muttered, rubbing the back of his neck. "If we could get a lead on what happened to it, we might be a little closer to finding out why we're being set up for a murder charge."

"'They knew,'" Tara murmured, remembering the dying man's last words again. "'The paintings were...'" She shook her head. "The paintings were what? Stolen? Everyone knew that."

Blake pulled absently at his lower lip, lost in thought.

Needing something to do—anything to distract her from Blake's admission that he'd found her attractive—Tara busied herself neatly repacking the duffel bag. The suit Blake had worn last evening. Her own dinner suit, now sadly crumpled.

She shook out the skirt, folded it, and laid it in the bag. And then she picked up the jacket. Remembering that she'd put her pearl necklace into one of the pockets, she felt a sudden need to make sure it was still safe. Maybe because she had so few of her own possessions with her, she needed to keep track of those she had. She plunged her hand into the left pocket, unable to recall which pocket she'd put the necklace in.

But rather than the strand of pearls, she pulled out a crumpled white envelope.

She stared at it blankly, knowing that it hadn't been there when she'd left for the art gallery. And suddenly she held it more gingerly, as if it might explode in her hand.

"Tara? What's wrong? What's that in your hand?" she heard Blake ask from behind her.

She turned to find him watching her closely.

"I found this in my jacket pocket," she said. "It wasn't there when I put the suit on."

Blake frowned and looked hard at the envelope. "You're sure?"

"I'm positive. I don't know where it came from."

"Do you mind if I see it?"

She handed it to him. He turned it over a couple of times, studying it. As far as Tara could see, it was a sealed, legal-size envelope with no markings on the outside.

Blake took a penknife from his pocket and carefully slit the seal. As Tara watched, he pulled out two sheets of paper and scanned them intently.

A moment later, he muttered a curse. "Where did this come from?"

"I told you, I don't know. I found it in my jacket pocket just now. I have no idea who put it there, or when."

Blake looked up from the papers, his gaze intent on her face. "You said you knelt beside the man on the floor. Could he have put it in your pocket then?"

Tara remembered the man groping weakly at her jacket as he lay beside her. Could he?

She covered her mouth with her hand, suddenly remembering something else—Botkin's lingering pat on her hip that she'd found so puzzling and offensive. But then she'd forgotten all about it when she'd found the same man lying in his own blood on the floor of the back office.

Blake eyed her expression closely. "You remembered something?"

She nodded. "I think Botkin put it in my pocket when we were looking at that ugly brown-and-yellow painting. I, er, I thought he was patting my butt. Apparently, he was slipping this into my pocket."

"You thought he was..." Blake grinned fleetingly, then his face became sober. "So he put this in your pocket before the time he was supposed to meet me in that hallway. Which could mean that he suspected he was being watched."

Tara bit her lip, remembering the man's dying words. *They knew.*

"Tell me what that is," she ordered Blake, nodding toward the contents of the envelope. "Tell me what it means."

"It means," he answered quietly, "that you and I are going to Savannah."

"Savannah? The city?" she repeated blankly.

He lifted an eyebrow. "You know another one?"

"Well, yes, as a matter of fact, but never mind that. Why are we going to Savannah?"

"I'll tell you on the way," he promised. "Let's pack up."

TARA WAITED until they were settled again into Blake's pickup truck before saying, "Now tell me what was in the envelope, and why we're going to Savannah."

"What would you say," Blake asked, instead, "if I told you I have reason to believe that the paintings stolen from Jackson Willfort's apartment in Atlanta were fakes?"

"The paintings he was going to put on display? The ones he bought from the Pryce Gallery?"

Blake nodded.

Tara frowned. "I suppose the first thing I would wonder, considering what the dying man said to me, is who, exactly, knew they were fakes. And then I would ask what the chances are that the robbery was staged for the purpose of insurance fraud—especially after what Spider told us about them not showing up in the usual places where stolen goods are fenced."

"The legal mind," Blake murmured admiringly. "Those are both very good questions."

Tara could probably have come up with several interesting scenarios, but she decided that would be a waste of time at the moment. "*Do* you have reason to believe the paintings were fakes?"

"If the papers I found in that envelope are legitimate, then yes, I do."

"So someone in the gallery—presumably the man who was killed—knew the paintings were frauds and contacted someone in the insurance company, who contacted you."

"And someone else found out, and killed him for it. The killer was probably searching Botkin's pockets when you came into the room and interrupted him."

"Not that it would have done him any good, anyway."

"Right. Because Botkin had already passed the papers to you, without your knowledge."

Tara chewed her lower lip. "So we're on our way to find out whether Willfort was involved."

"Basically," he agreed.

"Wouldn't it be more logical for us to stay in Atlanta? Liz Pryce is in Atlanta. The forged paintings came from her gallery. The paintings were stolen from Willfort's Atlanta apartment. Your informant was murdered in the gallery."

"Atlanta is too hot for us right now. There are too many people looking for us there, including, most likely, the police. I have a feeling we'll find some answers in Savannah."

"These, er, feelings of yours. How reliable are they?"

"Very."

"But they didn't tell you something was going to go wrong at the gallery last night."

He grimaced. "No."

"So they aren't infallible."

"I never said I was infallible."

"What are we going to do when we get to Savannah?"

"We'll figure that out when we get there," he answered, not looking overly concerned about their lack of a plan.

"Do you mind if I turn on the radio?"

"Help yourself."

It was going to be a long ride to Savannah, Tara thought as she turned the knob in search of decent music. And she didn't want to spend it daydreaming about how cozy the inside of the pickup was with the rain pounding the windshield and Blake's arm only inches from her own.

It would be easier to keep her emotional distance from him if she considered him nothing more than a temporary friend. They had been thrown together by circumstances, that was all. She fully intended to keep that fact in mind.

AFTER MORE THAN an hour on the road, they stopped for a short break at a fast-food restaurant in a little town somewhere off I-16. It felt good to get out of the truck and stretch. The rain had stopped, and the skies were clearing. Tara wanted to believe that was a good sign.

Tara made use of the ladies' room, then requested a diet soda in the restaurant. Blake ordered a towering ice cream, cake and fudge combination with a regular soda on the side. Tara watched in amazement as he put away the dessert, and remembered the bacon cheeseburger with fries he'd had for lunch. How on earth did he stay so lanky-slim if he ate this way?

He grinned sheepishly when she finally asked the question. "Metabolism," he replied. "I try to eat healthy most of the time, but every once in a while I gotta have a burger or ice cream."

Once again, she thought she heard a faint twang of Texas underneath his usually hard-to-place accent. "Where did you grow up, Blake?"

He shrugged. "All over. My family traveled a lot."

"How long have you lived in Georgia?"

He dipped a spoon into his dessert. "Who said I live in Georgia?"

She blinked. "You mean you don't?"

"Only occasionally."

She thought of that old motel in Marietta. "Where do you live when you aren't in this state?"

"Here and there."

"You don't have a permanent home anywhere?"

"I work out of Texas fairly often. Got a little place in the Tennessee hills where I sometimes go between jobs."

It sounded to Tara like a lonely existence. "You have no family?"

"I'm pretty much on my own."

There were so many more questions Tara wanted to ask him. Why he lived the way he did. Why he felt the need to have trucks stashed in used-car lots, motels booked under false names, why he apparently lived a footloose life with no ties to a home, a family or even possessions. But she knew those questions were none of her business, and that Blake would only tell her if he wanted her to know.

So, instead, she frowned and adopted a lighter tone.

"Blake, has anyone ever told you that you're just a bit strange?"

He grinned. "I believe 'weird' is the usual adjective."

"And that doesn't bother you?"

"I've gotten used to it. You sure you don't want any ice cream or anything?"

"No, I'm fine."

"Then we'd better be on our way."

The more she learned about Blake, the less she felt she knew him, Tara reflected as they climbed back into the black pickup. And the more he intrigued her.

IT HAD BEEN YEARS since Tara had visited Savannah. She had almost forgotten how beautiful it was, with its cobblestone streets and spreading magnolia trees, its historic houses and abundantly blooming azaleas.

She climbed out of the truck gratefully that evening, stiff from the hours on the road. She looked curiously around the beautifully landscaped grounds of the condominium complex in which Blake had parked. "Where are we?"

"A friend owns a condo here. She travels a lot, and she's out of town now, but I have her permission to stay here whenever I like."

She. Tara was a bit surprised by her immediate reaction to the pronoun. By the questions that flooded her mind. Questions that were absolutely none of her business.

Concentrate on what you're doing, Tara.

"You, er, have a key?" she asked him a bit too casually.

"Yes. She gave me one for emergencies like this."

Obviously, Blake didn't lead quite as lonely a life as Tara had imagined. And, obviously, she'd been foolish to start weaving romantic fantasies around the things he'd said to her earlier. He certainly didn't seem to have been pining for *her!*

Fifteen minutes later, she and Blake entered a beautifully furnished condominium with a breathtaking view of the Savannah River. Through the glass wall at the back of the white-on-white living room, Tara could see the lights from boats reflecting off the water.

"This is lovely," she murmured.

Blake looked very much at home as he tossed his cowboy hat on a low table. "Stephanie's done all right for herself."

Stephanie. "It's, um, very kind of her to let us stay here."

Blake nodded. "Listen, I'm going to take a shower and change before I start making calls. Make yourself at home, okay? I'm sure there are soft drinks and juice in the fridge. There's a TV hidden in that cabinet if you want to put your feet up and catch the news."

Tara didn't turn on the TV, nor did she raid the refrigerator after Blake disappeared somewhere into the condo. Instead, she unlocked and opened the glass doors and stepped out onto the balcony, where she could enjoy the rain-cooled evening and think about everything that had happened.

She didn't realize how much time passed while she stood there. She jumped when Blake spoke from behind her. "Nice out here, isn't it?"

"Yes, it's..."

She turned, and her words died in her throat when she saw that he was wearing a loose-fitting blue shirt, pleated gray slacks and gray suspenders. He'd even changed his shoes, from the pointed-toe cowboy boots he'd worn with his jeans, to black loafers. There was no doubt the clothes were his. And they hadn't been in the duffel bag he'd brought with them.

She twisted her hands in front of her and held on to her smile with a massive effort. ''Yes,'' she said again. ''It's lovely.''

Blake leaned against the door frame, arms crossed over his chest, legs crossed at the ankles. The soft light from a fixture beside the door illuminated him in a golden glow. Just looking at him made Tara's pulse race.

''I'd like to take you out to dinner,'' he said.

Her eyebrows rose. ''That's how I got into trouble the last time.''

His smile was forced. ''I know. And this is another working meal. We're meeting someone.''

''Another one of your strange friends?''

''I'm afraid so.''

Questions swirling in her head, she smoothed her hands over her discount-store jeans. ''I hope we're not going anywhere too elegant,'' she murmured, feeling underdressed compared to Blake.

''You'll want to change.''

''Well, I have the dinner suit I wore yesterday,'' she said. ''It's badly wrinkled, but surely there's an iron or a steamer here.''

He shook his head. ''We'll find you something here.

You and Stephanie are about the same size, though she's probably a couple of inches taller."

"Blake, I am not raiding your friend's closet." Tara was appalled at the very idea.

"She won't mind."

She shook her head. "No."

Blake reached out, took her hand, and threaded their fingers together in that cozy, intimate, enticing way that he had. "Come on," he said. "Let's go find you something to wear."

"Really, Blake, I—"

But he was already moving, dragging her with him, talking nonstop with teasing nonsense intended to keep her off balance. He steered her through a frilly, peach-and-mint bedroom and into a closet that was bigger than Tara's entire bedroom in Atlanta. She stopped in her tracks, her jaw dropping.

She'd never seen so many clothes in her life. Silks, satins, sequins. Casual clothes, sporty clothes, evening clothes. What appeared to be hundreds of pairs of shoes neatly arranged in a wall full of cubicles. Clear plastic drawers stuffed with scarves and other accessories. Hatboxes stacked on the upper shelves.

"Your, er, friend likes clothes," she said weakly, aware of the inanity of her understatement.

Blake was already rummaging among the racks. "Comes with the career. She's a model."

Of course she was, Tara thought grimly. "Still, Blake, we can't just help ourselves to her clothing. That's going beyond the bounds of simple hospitality."

"Trust me, she won't mind. Would you like me to call her and let her tell you personally?"

"No! I mean—"

He turned away from the clothing and took both her hands, held them in front of him and gave her a melting smile. "Sweetheart, I really don't have time to go shopping again right now. Just wear something of Stephanie's this evening and we'll try to pick you up some more things tomorrow, okay?"

He made it sound so logical. As if it would be completely childish and unreasonable of her to refuse. And the way he was holding her hands and looking so deeply into her eyes scrambled all her mental circuits, making it impossible to remember her reasons for arguing with him.

Tara sighed. "All right. Just for tonight."

He brushed his lips across her knuckles, sending a tingle all the way to her toes. Their gazes locked over their linked hands, and Tara's breath caught in her throat. Her lips parted involuntarily, waiting for a kiss that seemed inevitable.

And then Blake dropped her hands and turned briskly back to the clothing. "Okay, we're looking for something nice but not overly dressy. A pantsuit is probably out, considering that her legs are about a mile longer than yours—"

Still breathless from that moment of purely sexual awareness, Tara winced at this reminder of where they were, and why.

Blake extracted an emerald-green knit dress from the crowded rack. It would probably be a mini on long-legged Stephanie, but it looked to be about average length for Tara. And the stretch-knit fabric made size less important.

She nodded reluctantly. "It's pretty."

"Steph wears a lot of green. It looks good with her red hair."

Tara told herself it was incredibly petty, catty and immature of her to dislike a woman she'd never even met. Especially one who had opened her home to them and was sharing her wardrobe—whether she knew it or not. The fact that her dislike was caused by the undisguised affection in Blake's voice every time he mentioned the woman only increased her self-disgust.

Blake was already rummaging among the shoes. "You wear a seven-and-a-half, right?"

He should know, since he'd bought the sneakers she was now wearing. She nodded.

"Hmm. Steph's got a big foot. A ten."

"I have my own shoes," Tara said quickly. "The black pumps I wore last night are in your truck."

"I'll get them while you change. Take a shower if you like. Everything you should need is in the bathroom."

When she stepped into the peach-and-mint bath attached to the master bedroom a few minutes later, Tara was overcome by a sense of rather reckless expectation that startled her. Who'd have thought she could actually be excited about going out in borrowed clothes to investigate an art theft that might be connected to a murder?

Living on the run, cut off from her friends, family and all her possessions, never knowing what was going to happen next—she should be hating every minute of this. It surprised her that she wasn't. She felt more alive than she had since she'd been cut adrift

The Editor's "Thank You" Free Gifts Include:
- **Two BRAND-NEW romance novels!**
- **An exciting mystery gift!**

PLACE
FREE GIFT
SEAL
HERE

YES! I have placed my Editor's "Thank You" seal in the space provided above. Please send me 2 free books and an exciting mystery gift. I understand I am under no obligation to purchase any books, as explained on the back and on the opposite page.

142 HDL CF3E (U-H-T-03/98)

Name

Address   Apt.

City

State   Zip

Thank You!

DETACH AND MAIL CARD TODAY!

If offer card is missing write to: Harlequin Reader Service, 3010 Walden Ave., P.O. Box 1867, Buffalo, NY 14240-1867

BUSINESS REPLY MAIL
FIRST-CLASS MAIL   PERMIT NO. 717   BUFFALO, NY

POSTAGE WILL BE PAID BY ADDRESSEE

HARLEQUIN READER SERVICE
3010 WALDEN AVE
PO BOX 1867
BUFFALO NY 14240-9952

NO POSTAGE
NECESSARY
IF MAILED
IN THE
UNITED STATES

from the law firm where she'd expected to be until retirement. And she knew that at least part of that exhilaration was due to Blake.

She wondered half-seriously if everything she'd been through lately had affected her reasoning. Because where Blake was concerned, it was becoming increasingly difficult to be the cautious and sensible woman she'd always considered herself to be.

7

WEARING the borrowed green knit dress and her black pumps—without stockings, since hers had been ruined and she'd refused to delve into Stephanie's lingerie—Tara followed Blake into a small, but expensive-looking Italian restaurant later that evening. He still hadn't explained exactly who they were meeting. When she'd pressed him, he'd said only that it was an old friend who might have some information for them.

Blake's friend wasn't there when they arrived, so he obtained a table for them in the very back of the dim, candlelit room, informing the hostess that they were expecting someone to join them. He ordered white wine while they waited.

"Just so you're prepared, my friend is a bit...odd," Blake said when the wine had been delivered, sampled and approved. He grinned as he spoke, letting her know that he was intentionally repeating his earlier warning about Spider.

Tara made a face. "At least we're meeting in nicer surroundings this time."

Blake smiled, then narrowed his eyes. "Here's Perry now."

The man was tall and quite thin, with shaggy, sandy hair and deep-set eyes. He wore a short-sleeved black shirt, black jeans and scuffed black boots. Something about him made Tara's mental warning systems sound...the systems she'd developed during her years working with the IRS.

She'd met more than a few con men in her life. And her gut instinct told her that she was about to meet another one.

Blake stood and stuck out his right hand. The other man gripped it warmly. It was obvious that there was a bond between them.

The men exchanged rapid greetings, indulged in a few moments of conversation that seemed to consist primarily of obscure references and impossible-to-follow half sentences, then turned to Tara.

"Tara, this is Perry." Blake didn't add surnames, but seemed to think his introduction sufficient.

Tara held out her right hand. Perry lifted it to his lips, the gesture reminding her of Blake, though her reaction to it was entirely different. If she'd had her purse with her, she'd have pulled it a bit closer to her.

"Blake told me he had a lady friend with him, but he didn't mention how beautiful she was," Perry drawled in the accent of the deepest South. An accent Tara knew well from her childhood in tiny Honoria, Georgia. She'd made a halfhearted effort to lessen her own while she'd studied at Harvard, having learned early on that a Southern accent was often mistaken for an intellectual deficiency.

She murmured something noncommittal in response to his balderdash and glanced at Blake for a clue about how to handle the guy.

"Have a seat, Perry," Blake said. "Would you like some wine? Are you hungry?"

Draping his long frame into a chair, Perry gave Blake a lazy, one-sided grin. "Son, you know I'm always hungry. I'll just about eat anything that don't bite me first."

He seemed determined to prove his words when he placed his order. It was all Tara could do not to react when Perry practically read the entire menu to the young man who waited on their table. He began with a large appetizer, moved on to soup, ordered an entrée with several side dishes, and then announced that he would choose his dessert later. From the way Blake winced each time Perry made another extravagant selection, Tara assumed that her partner would be picking up the check.

Perry, it turned out, wasn't one to talk while he ate. He gave his entire concentration to his meal, leaving small talk to Blake and Tara while he shoveled food into his thin body with an enthusiasm that left Tara amazed. Apparently aware of his friend's habits, Blake didn't even try to engage the other man in serious conversation until Perry's plates had been emptied, dessert served and coffee poured. Only then did Perry seem to relax enough to be talkative.

"So, Perry, how've you been?" Blake asked.

"Fair to middlin'."

"Still working the circuit?"

"Now and again."

"Circuit?" Tara looked curiously from Blake to Perry. "Rodeo?"

Perry chuckled. "Not exactly."

Blake cleared his throat.

Her earlier suspicions kicking in again, Tara frowned.

"I'm what some folks might call a grifter, ma'am," Perry said unapologetically.

"A con man," she said with a sigh.

"That's another term for it," he agreed.

"Tara," Blake murmured, "is a lawyer."

Perry's eyebrows rose in interest. "Yeah? I've had some dealings with lawyers. You might say we're in the same line of work, I reckon."

Tara's eyes widened. She was getting rather tired of Blake's questionable friends casting aspersions on her profession. "I would certainly *not* say that."

Blake's grin made her long to kick his shin beneath the table.

"If it makes you feel any better, I don't take the life savings of senior citizens," Perry offered. "A little three-card monte, a few variations on the shell game, but mostly I make my living hustlin' cards and pool."

"Perry's a good friend, Tara. I'd trust him with my life," Blake added simply.

She softened. "I'm not presuming to judge you, Perry. You're here this evening to help us, and I appreciate that."

"No offense taken, Miz Tara," he assured her, stretching the syllables as far as they'd go.

Blake nodded and got down to business. "I told you a bit of our situation on the phone this afternoon," he said to Perry.

Perry nodded. "Sounds like y'all've got yourself into a heap of trouble."

Tara was beginning to wonder if Perry used that

Southern accent like a disguise, hiding his real thoughts behind platitudes and clichés. She'd like to know how he and Blake had become such good friends.

Something told her there was an interesting story behind that meeting.

"What can you tell me that I don't already know about Jack Willfort?" Blake asked Perry.

Perry shrugged. "Rumor has it that he's planning a run for office during the next election."

"I've heard that one."

"Rumor has it that he's going to play heavily on his rep as a solid family man, a rock of the community, a real straight arrow."

"C'mon, man, I need something I don't already know."

"Rumor has it," Perry murmured, stirring his coffee, "that he's been bangin' a rich, married society lady in Atlanta for more'n a few years."

Blake's left eyebrow shot upward. "Is that so?"

"Like I said, that's the scoop."

Blake's eyes met Tara's across the table.

"Liz Pryce?" she whispered.

Blake looked to Perry, who shrugged. "Don't have any names, bud, just talk."

"Any more where that came from?"

Perry cleared his throat. "Maybe."

Grinning wryly, Blake slid something across the table to his friend, who picked it up and pocketed it without glancing at it. "I've heard there's a couple of paintings in his collection that shouldn't ought to be there."

"And where ought they to be?"

Perry shrugged. "Wherever someone might fence stolen paintings. They got a pawn shop for stuff like that?"

Blake glanced swiftly around them, then leaned closer to the other man. "Are you saying the paintings were never stolen?"

"Man, I'm only passin' along some street talk. What you make of it is up to you."

Perry drained his coffee cup and then pushed away from the table. "If y'all will excuse me, I've got an appointment this evening. Blake, it's been good to see you again."

The two men solemnly shook hands. And then Perry took Tara's hand and lifted it once again to his lips. This time he lingered a bit longer over the gesture.

"Ma'am," he said when he released her hand. "It's been a real pleasure."

"It was very nice to meet you, Perry."

He left the restaurant without a backward glance.

Tara let out a deep breath and looked quizzically at Blake. "What did you give him?"

"Let's just say I staked his poker game tonight."

She blinked. "Your friend charged you for his information?"

Blake lifted a shoulder. "A man's gotta make a living."

Remembering the bill Blake had left in that warehouse for Spider, Tara reflected that Blake's friends certainly seemed expensive. She only hoped the information they were passing along was worth whatever it was costing him.

BACK IN Stephanie's condo, Tara kicked off her shoes and began to pace as she tried to put all the pieces of their puzzle together. "Liz Pryce and Jackson Willfort are having an affair," she began.

Leaning back against a built-in bookcase, Blake crossed his arms over his chest and watched her. "We don't know that for certain," he cautioned her.

"Right. But if they are, think how much damage it could do to both of them if the word got out. Willfort's supposedly a conservative, morally superior family man. Liz Pryce is married to an extremely powerful man who could crush her and cause Willfort a lot of trouble. Both of them would probably go to any lengths to keep their affair quiet."

"Their alleged affair, counselor."

Ignoring his teasing gibe, Tara paced on, deep in thought. "You have paperwork to indicate the stolen paintings were fakes. Perry's heard a rumor that the paintings never left Willfort's collection. Someone from the insurance company carrying the policy on the stolen paintings contacted you and directed you to the gallery, but now you can't reach that person. Who called you, and was it his intention all along to frame you?"

"Good questions."

"Yes, with no answers. So how are we going to..." She came to an abrupt halt, staring at Blake. "What are you doing?"

A glass paperweight, a brass dog, and a marble apple—all items from the shelves Blake leaned against—seemed to be dancing in the air above his busy hands.

While Tara watched, the items arced, fell, rose and tumbled in ever-changing patterns.

"I'm juggling," he answered matter-of-factly, eyes on the objects.

"Why?"

"I think better this way."

"Oh." She found his movements strangely fascinating. She watched for a few more moments, then asked, "Do you have any other hidden talents?"

His grin was downright sinful. "A few."

For some reason, her cheeks went scarlet. She turned away to hide her face. "What are we going to do now?" she asked, making a pretense of looking out the window to admire the moonlight glittering on the inky-black river.

She heard Blake set the items back on the shelves. "We're going to bed," he replied.

She turned quickly. Surely he didn't mean...

His expression was blandly innocent. "Neither of us got much sleep last night," he added. "We'll both think more clearly when we've had some rest. I'll take the spare bedroom. You can have Stephanie's room."

He seemed to enjoy flustering her. It annoyed her that he did it so easily. She'd always considered herself immune to innuendos and double entendres. She'd certainly heard enough of them in her time, and she never allowed herself to blush like a schoolgirl.

She didn't like the thought of using the other woman's bed. And she hated the haunting mental images of Blake sharing it with a leggy redhead.

You really are going to have to stop doing this, Tara, she warned herself.

"Maybe you should take the master bedroom," she said. "After all, she is your friend."

Blake shook his head. "I always use the spare when I visit," he replied. "I sort of consider it my room."

His words only confused Tara further about his relationship with the absent Stephanie.

"You'll need something to sleep in," he said. "Steph has nightgowns somewhere in that monster closet."

"Would you mind very much if I use your sweat suit again?" Tara asked instead. "It was, um, comfortable."

His smile held a tender edge that made her hands quiver. "No, sweetheart. I don't mind at all," he assured her. "I'll get it for you."

It took her the entire four minutes he was gone to recover from that smile, and the casually spoken endearment.

This was no way to keep her emotional distance from Blake.

Blake returned carrying the sweat suit and a clean pair of white socks. He handed them to Tara, then asked, "Is there anything else you need?"

"No, I'm fine, thanks."

He seemed suddenly reluctant to send her off. "You'll be okay in there by yourself?"

Tara made a face at him. "I've been sleeping by myself for a long time, Blake."

That lifted one of his eyebrows a bit, but he merely nodded. "I just thought—well, with everything that's been happening, it would certainly be understandable if you were a bit nervous."

"I'm fine," she repeated.

"You'll let me know if you need anything?"

"You'll be the first to know," she assured him dryly. As if there was anyone else to tell.

"And if you have another bad dream—"

"Blake," she interrupted him. "I'm fine. Really. There won't be any more bad dreams."

"You're sure?"

"I'm sure. Now go to bed. Get some rest."

He leaned over to brush a kiss across her lips. "Good night, Tara."

"Good night, Blake." Her reply was noticeably husky.

"TARA."

The sound of her name penetrated her dream. She opened her eyes, then almost groaned at the sight of Blake sitting on the side of the big bed. The room was gray, but there was enough light for her to see him clearly. His hair was tousled and he wore nothing but a pair of dark-colored sweatpants.

She dragged her gaze away from his sleek, bare chest. The details of her dream came back all too clearly to her, making her face flame. "Please tell me I didn't talk in my sleep again," she croaked.

He stroked her hair away from her face, his fingers warm against her chilled skin. "No. You just seemed restless. I was afraid you were having another nightmare."

It hadn't been a nightmare. But Tara had no intention of telling Blake exactly what type of dream it *had* been, nor that he had played a prominent role in it.

"What time is it?" she asked.

"A little after six."

She grimaced. "I'm sorry, Blake. I keep disturbing your sleep."

"In more ways than you think," he murmured, his fingers lingering on her cheek.

She swallowed and reached hastily for the glass of water she'd placed on the nightstand during the night. Aware of Blake's eyes on her, she drank half of it, the liquid loosening her tight throat.

"Better?" Blake asked, taking the glass from her and setting it back on the nightstand.

She nodded. "I was thirsty."

He brushed a drop of water from her lower lip with his thumb. Her mouth tingled in response to his touch. The erotic dream echoed in her mind as she gazed up at Blake, aware that they were alone in an intimately shadowed bedroom, that he sat only inches from where she lay. That it would take only a sign from her to have him crawl in beside her.

Holding her gaze with his, he traced her jaw with his fingertips, then her chin. And then her lower lip again, which quivered beneath his touch. "How can you look so good this early in the morning?" he asked whimsically.

"I—er—" Now, how was she supposed to answer that?

"I keep telling myself," Blake mused, "that it would be wrong of me to take advantage of you when you have no choice but to be with me, through no fault of your own. But you make it very difficult for me to keep my hands to myself, beautiful Tara McBride."

Tara had never considered herself beautiful. Her cousin, Savannah, was the beauty of the McBride family. Their cousin Emily was pretty, in a sweet, wholesome, girl-next-door way. Tara was just…Tara. Intelligent. Competent. Attractive enough in her neat, professional manner. But beautiful? No.

But the way Blake was looking at her now, as he leaned over her, the way he touched her…he made her feel beautiful. And the sensation was a heady one.

He was the beautiful one, she couldn't help thinking. His chest and arms were so firm, so muscled. She couldn't resist reaching out to touch him. Her hand skimmed up his left arm to hesitate at his shoulder. He felt even better than he looked, she decided.

Blake leaned closer. "I would really like to kiss you, Tara," he murmured.

She really wanted him to do so. But still she was afraid of getting too close. Of wanting too much. Of failing again.

She didn't try to stop him when he brushed his lips lightly across hers. And she didn't push him away when he kissed her again.

His lips settled firmly on hers, this kiss bolder, more peremptory than the ones that had preceded it. As if each time he kissed her, he felt that he had more right to do so. And maybe he did, she couldn't help thinking as she responded to the kiss with less hesitation than she'd felt before.

Bracing himself on his forearms, Blake deepened the kiss, pressing her into the pillows, his body almost touching hers. Beneath the soft, thick fleece of her borrowed sweat suit, her breasts felt ultra-sensitized, aching for his touch. She could almost feel the warmth of him, and she wanted very badly to reach up and pull him down the rest of the way, until there was no distance at all remaining between them.

He murmured something into her mouth. His hand cupped her cheek, tilting her head to a new angle against the pillow. He kissed her as though he were starving for her taste.

Sliding without resistance into temptation, Tara returned the kiss with an equal fervor. Exactly the way she'd been wanting to kiss him for longer than she was ready to admit.

Her hand slid over his shoulder to stroke his back. His muscles rippled beneath her touch. He groaned, deep in his chest.

A thick ridge of scar tissue just below his left shoulder blade bunched beneath her fingertips. Blake froze suddenly, then lifted his head, breaking off the kiss.

A moment later, he was on his feet beside the bed, his hands clenched at his sides. Tara noted dazedly that his hands weren't steady.

What had she done that had made him draw back so abruptly?

"Go back to sleep if you like," he said gruffly, avoiding her questioning eyes. "I tend to be an early riser, anyway, and I have some things I want to do this morning."

As if she'd be able to sleep now!

"I—" She had to clear her throat before she could complete the sentence. "I think I'd rather get up."

Blake nodded, turned, and headed out of the room as though he was being urgently paged from somewhere else. "Help yourself to whatever you need," he said over his shoulder. "Stephanie won't mind."

Stephanie.

How could Tara have forgotten about the other woman? The one in whose bed she was lying. The one in whose bed Blake had probably already lain.

Tara slid out of the bed and ran her trembling hands through her hair.

She was an idiot. No doubt about it. She was falling for a juggling P.I. who didn't seem to believe in last names, who had no permanent address, who kept clothes in the apartment of a redheaded model whose legs were "a mile longer" than Tara's. Only a fool would let herself become too attached to a man like that.

It was only proximity, she tried to tell herself. She had no one else to turn to right now. Her dependence on him was certainly understandable, she assured herself.

And he was an exceptionally good-looking man. Intriguingly mysterious. Engagingly unpredictable. Charming. Any normal, healthy woman would find herself drawn to him under the circumstances.

What she had to do was to keep reminding herself that this was only temporary. That they were the wrong man and the wrong woman brought together at the wrong time. She could not allow herself to be tempted to forget the warnings of her common sense.

Not if she wanted to emerge from this experience with both her body and her heart intact.

TARA TOOK a long shower, then brushed her teeth, dried her hair, and applied what little makeup she had. She dressed in the jeans she'd worn the day before and the clean red-and-white T-shirt. She took her time making the bed she'd slept in, trying to arrange the ruffled throw pillows the way they'd been before.

She accidentally bumped against the nightstand when she moved back from the bed, knocking over a tiny antique-brass picture frame. When she set it upright, Blake's face smiled up at her. It was a snapshot taken several years earlier, apparently. His longish, gold-tipped hair was ruffled by the wind, and his smile was bright and carefree. He was looking at the person holding the camera with obvious affection.

Tara set the little frame down as if it had suddenly burned her fingers.

How much more evidence did Tara need to convince her that she couldn't take Blake's flirting seriously?

No matter how badly she might have wanted to.

GIVING LITTLE THOUGHT to his choices, Blake dragged a long-sleeved green shirt and a pair of khaki chinos out of the closet in Stephanie's spare bedroom and threw them on. His hair was still wet from the long, cold shower he'd taken after leaving Tara. He styled it by running a hand through it.

Shoving his bare feet into a pair of leather deck shoes, he told himself that he had to get out for a while. He suspected that Tara would want to go with him, but he hoped he could convince her to stay here. She would be safe here. And he could use the time away from her to remember all the reasons it wouldn't be right for him to get involved with her.

The scar her exploring fingers had discovered on his back—the one that had been caused by an insane man's bullet—was only one reminder of the differences between them. She had the kind of past Blake had only fantasized about, a future ahead of her that he could never fit into. And he doubted that she was the type of woman who would be content with a few nights of no-strings pleasure, to be followed by a genial goodbye.

Blake didn't know how to offer anything more.

BLAKE WAS SITTING at the kitchen table with a cup of coffee and the newspaper when Tara entered. He looked up to smile at her when she entered the room. She noticed immediately that his smile wasn't reflected in his eyes. She could almost see the wall he'd put up between them.

What had changed during that kiss? What had made him suddenly draw away from her? She couldn't help wondering if Stephanie had anything to do with Blake's sudden reserve.

"What we have to do," Blake said without preface, "is to get into Jackson Willfort's mansion and get a look at his private art collection."

Tara sank heavily into a chair. "You want to break into Willfort's mansion?" she asked faintly, thinking of magazine photographs she'd seen of the heavily guarded modern fortress and trying to imagine herself dressed in black and scaling barbed-wire-topped walls. "Don't you think that's dangerous—especially if Willfort is backing the people who are looking for us?"

"I didn't say we have to break in," he corrected her, looking back down at the newspaper with a thoughtful expression. "I said we have to *get* in."

"I suppose you expect us to ring the bell and say, 'Pardon us, Mr. Willfort, do you mind if we look through your private collection to see if you have a couple of pieces that might have accidentally been reported stolen?'"

Blake gave her a look in response to her sarcasm. "That wasn't exactly what I had in mind."

"Why do I have the feeling that you have a plan? And that I'm not going to like it?"

He grinned. "Seems like I'm not the only one who has fairly reliable instincts."

And then his grin faded. He reached out and took a strand of her blond hair between his fingers.

"Have you ever wondered," he asked whimsically, "how it would feel to be a redhead?"

"I—er—"

His smile turned devilish. "Trust me, Tara. You're going to look great."

8

BLAKE WOULDN'T tell Tara exactly what he had in mind. "I'm not keeping anything from you," he assured her. "I just need to work out the details a bit more before I discuss it with you, okay?"

When he left the apartment later that morning, telling her he would be back soon, she tried to argue. She reminded him that she was a partner in this escapade, not a bystander. She wouldn't be treated like excess baggage, she asserted.

He refused to listen. Telling her that what he had to do had to be done alone, he left her alone in Stephanie's apartment. She paced angrily for a few minutes after the door closed behind him, furious with him for shutting her out now, yet still foolishly aching for the feel of his arms around her.

She was an idiot, she thought in annoyance.

She suddenly wanted very badly to talk to someone who loved her. Odd that when she'd been able to call her family anytime during the last couple of weeks, she'd deliberately avoided doing so. Now that calling them was riskier, she was almost overwhelmed by the urge.

She told herself it couldn't possibly be dangerous to call from here. No one except Stephanie knew she and

Blake were staying here, and Blake obviously trusted Stephanie implicitly.

It was ridiculous to think that anyone would be monitoring her parents' phone...wasn't it? Just because whoever had chased them to Marietta knew exactly who she was didn't mean they would be watching her family...did it?

At what point did reasonable precautions become rampant paranoia?

She could call her brother Trevor in Washington. But Trevor had always known her too well. He'd hear her voice and immediately know that something was wrong, which was one reason she'd avoided calling him after she'd been fired from the law firm.

Trevor was the type who thought he had to take care of everything. That was one of the reasons he was so drawn to politics. He would have been immediately on the phone to her former employers, demanding that they reinstate her immediately. And if he knew that she'd become involved in a murder, he would be on a plane to Georgia within the hour.

As for her younger brother, Trent—well, he was young. And he tended to worry too much. Calling him would serve no purpose except to upset him.

But the silence in a stranger's apartment was pressing down on her, making her feel much more alone than she'd been during those two weeks she'd holed up to sulk in her own apartment. After another hour of pacing, trying without success to get interested in one of Stephanie's books, and staring out the window at the river, Tara could resist no longer. She needed to talk to someone, or go crazy.

She picked up the phone and dialed the number of the one person who never failed to be available when she was needed. As young as she was, Emily McBride was the best listener in the family, the one whose doors, and whose heart, were always open.

"Tara, it's so good to hear from you," Emily said warmly, immediately identifying her cousin's voice. "I've been worried about you."

"Worried about me?" Tara was surprised. "Why?"

"I could tell at Dad's funeral that something was really bothering you. And no one's heard from you since you left town. Aunt Bobbie and Uncle Caleb are afraid you've been working too hard. Aunt Bobbie's been hoping you would call her soon. Have you talked to her today?"

Tara didn't realize she'd given her parents any reason to fret about her. "No, I haven't called Mom today," she admitted. "Emily, will you do me a favor?"

"Of course. What is it?"

"Tell Mom you heard from me, and that I'll call her in a few days, okay? Maybe another week. Tell her I'm still on my business trip and I really don't have time to talk right now. Tell her I just called you to see how you're holding up, will you?"

There was a moment's hesitation, and then, "Tara, what's wrong?"

"It's a long story," Tara said, wondering if she'd made a mistake calling her cousin. "I'm sort of in a mess right now, but I'm all right. I just wanted to talk to someone for a minute."

"Can you tell me what happened?"

"No. I'm afraid not. But don't try to call my apartment, okay? I won't be there for a while. Tell Mom *not* to call there. I'll call her, just as soon as I can."

"Does this have something to do with your work? Have you gotten involved in a difficult case?"

"Something like that," Tara answered, feeling guilty for the lie.

"You're...you're not in any actual danger or anything, are you?"

Tara faked a laugh. "Of course not. Really, Emily, don't worry about me, okay? I just called to find out how you are."

"I'm fine," Emily answered, not sounding noticeably reassured. "I've gotten lots of rest during the past couple of weeks. More than I've had in the past year, actually."

Tara knew that her cousin had had a difficult time of it, caring for her father who had died very slowly and very painfully. At only twenty-six, Emily had been forced to sacrifice a great deal, utterly refusing to put Uncle Josiah in a nursing home.

"You're still working every day?" Tara asked, thinking of how little time Emily had taken for herself. "Have you taken any time off since Uncle Junior died?"

"Only a couple days for the funeral arrangements," Emily admitted. "I'd like to take some time off, but it's been so busy at the office lately, and I hate to leave them in a bind. Maybe someday..."

Typical of Emily to be so aware of everyone else's problems, so oblivious to her own. Didn't she ever long to break away from her tiny hometown? To do something completely reckless and selfish and carefree, while she was still young?

But then, hadn't Tara basically given up her own youth in pursuit of her career goals? When was the last time *Tara* had done anything reckless and irresponsible, just for fun?

The adventure she was having right now didn't count, of course. Running for her life, sidestepping the law at every turn—well, it was hardly a carefree lark. And, yet, oddly enough, Tara had felt more animated and energetic during the past few hours than she had in weeks.

"You'll tell Mom I called? That I'm all right, and that I'll be in touch with her?" Tara repeated to Emily.

"I'll tell her. And, Tara, you'll call again if you need anything, won't you? You'd let us know if anything is really wrong?"

"Of course." She would have to call if she suddenly saw her face splashed across the television screen, Tara thought grimly.

It was a miracle, on the whole, that it hadn't already happened. And wouldn't the gossipy citizens of Honoria, Georgia love to hear that yet another McBride was suspected of murder: Emily's brother, Lucas, had left town under a similar cloud fifteen years ago, and hadn't been heard from since. Tara didn't want to have to disappear the way that Lucas had. Emily still grieved for her missing, much-older half brother. Tara couldn't bear to think of causing her own family the same heartache.

Tara heard a key in the lock of the front door and her

pulse increased. Blake had returned. "I have to go, Emily. Take care of yourself for a change, you hear?"

"You do the same."

"I'll try," Tara promised and hung up the phone.

She smoothed suddenly damp palms over the legs of her jeans as she turned to meet Blake, hoping she'd done the right thing by making the phone call.

It wasn't Blake who entered the room. It was a tall, stunningly beautiful redhead in a formfitting knit dress that ended above her knees to reveal shapely, mile-long legs. Tara immediately felt plain and dowdy in comparison to this vision of feminine perfection.

Stephanie, she thought, her heart sinking.

Could this situation get any more complicated?

"WHY, HELLO." Stephanie's pretty face lit up with what appeared to be a genuinely friendly smile. "You must be Tara."

"Yes. And you're Stephanie."

"That's right. Where's Blake?"

"He's gone out. He didn't say where."

Stephanie shook her head and sighed. "He rarely does."

"It was very kind of you to let us use your apartment this way," Tara offered, feeling awkward.

Stephanie brushed off her thanks. "Blake knows he and his friends are always welcome here. Are you hungry? I missed breakfast and I'm starving."

Tara glanced at her watch, realizing that it was nearly two in the afternoon. Just where was Blake, anyway?

Stephanie had already headed for the kitchen. "Do

you like spaghetti? I have homemade sauce in the freezer. It'll just take a few minutes to heat it up and boil some pasta to go with it. And there are probably some vegetables in the fridge for a salad."

It looked as though she and Stephanie were going to cook lunch together, Tara thought, dutifully following. How cozy.

"Blake told me he's gotten you involved in one of his cases," Stephanie said as she opened her freezer and peered inside. "I have to admit I was surprised. He's usually very careful not to endanger innocent bystanders."

Tara felt compelled, for some reason, to defend Blake. "He really had no idea that this case would turn dangerous. He never would have gotten me involved if he had."

Placing the frozen sauce in the microwave, Stephanie glanced at Tara, making Tara wonder just what the other woman had heard in her voice. "No, of course not," she agreed, sounding thoughtful.

There were so many questions Tara would have liked to ask Stephanie, and not one of them was any of her business, she reminded herself. Stephanie's relationship to Blake was of no concern to Tara—or so she wanted to believe.

"Is there anything I can do to help with lunch?" Tara asked quickly.

Stephanie nodded toward a cabinet door. "There's a big pan inside there. You can fill it with water and set it on to boil for the pasta while I cut up a salad."

As she complied, Tara wondered where Stephanie had grown up. Her accent reminded Tara of Blake's—

an intriguing mixture of the South and the Southwest. And again, she asked herself just how long Stephanie and Blake had known each other.

She turned to find Stephanie absently juggling three tomatoes on her way from the refrigerator to the island counter. The swift, skillful movements of Stephanie's hands as she tossed and caught the colorful fruit reminded Tara forcibly of Blake again.

Catching Tara watching her, Stephanie laughed a bit self-consciously and set the tomatoes carefully on the counter. "Dumb habit," she murmured. "I can hardly pick up more than two items at a time without juggling them. I blame it on Blake—he's always doing the same thing."

"So you've, um, known Blake a long time," Tara said, trying to sound nonchalant.

Stephanie lifted an eyebrow in apparent surprise. "You mean he hasn't told you...?"

"I see you two have met," Blake said, entering the kitchen at that moment.

The way Stephanie's face lit up at the sight of Blake made Tara's heart twist.

"Blake." Even Stephanie's voice had gone warm and soft as she stepped forward to greet him.

Tara watched from the corner of her eyes as Blake took Stephanie in his arms for a hug, and then gave her a smacking kiss on the cheek. "You look good," he said, holding her at arm's length for inspection.

Good? Tara had to resist making a face at the understatement. Anyone with two eyes couldn't help but notice that Stephanie was drop-dead gorgeous.

"And you aren't too hard on the eyes, either," Stephanie teased in return. "I hope you're hungry. Tara and I are making spaghetti for lunch."

Blake glanced at Tara, his expression suddenly a bit guarded, his smile changing. The memory of that morning kiss seemed to hang in the air between them.

"Spaghetti sounds good," Blake said. "Anything I can do to help?"

"Just stay out of the way," Stephanie replied, her green eyes darting from Blake to Tara and back again.

He obediently took a seat at the bar, close enough to talk with them, but out of the traffic pattern.

"You were gone a long time," Tara said to him, trying to make conversation—as opposed to just standing there gazing longingly at him. "Did you have a productive morning?"

"Somewhat," he agreed. "I think I'm getting closer to figuring out what happened. I'll know for certain when we get inside Willfort's house."

"Oh, my goodness," Stephanie murmured, dropping a carrot. "Is that really necessary, Blake?" she asked worriedly.

"I'm afraid so. But I have a plan."

Stephanie groaned and looked at Tara. "I usually run for cover when I hear him say those words," she advised. "Maybe you'd better do the same."

Blake smiled a little, but shook his head. "She can't. I need her."

Tara's heart gave a little jump in response to the words. She told it to behave. "What do you want me to do?" she asked calmly.

Instead of answering her directly, Blake looked at Stephanie. "Can you help us change her appearance?"

Stephanie looked speculatively at Tara. "In what way?"

"Can you turn her into one of Jeremy's girls?"

Stephanie's eyes widened. "So that's what you have in mind."

Tara wished she knew what the heck was going on. Who was Jeremy—a pimp? Just what, exactly, *was* Blake planning?

Blake nodded. "I've already talked to Jeremy. It's the best opportunity I'm going to get, Steph."

He'd left the morning newspaper lying on the table. He reached over to retrieve it and laid it on the island, pointing to an article in the "Lifestyles" section.

Tara leaned over to read the column, which focused on a major charity event to be held the following Friday evening at the spacious country estate of local millionaire philanthropist C. Jackson Willfort. The feature act, the article said, would be internationally famous magician Jeremy Kane. Tickets to the event were five hundred dollars per head, by invitation only, with proceeds to be donated to a local battered women's shelter. Two hundred guests were expected to attend.

"You're going to try to get us invitations?" Tara asked blankly.

"Not exactly," Blake murmured.

"He's planning to go in undercover," Stephanie explained, looking a bit concerned. "You as a magician's assistant. Himself as—what, Blake? A techie?"

He nodded. "Something like that."

Tara felt her eyes grow wide. "Me? A magician's assistant? One of Jeremy Kane's redheads? Blake, that's crazy!"

"This is the only way I know to find out for ourselves what's going on, Tara," he said. "I called my contact in Atlanta, and the police are still looking for a couple matching our descriptions in connection with the unsolved robbery of the Pryce Gallery. The police still don't have our real names—probably because the men who shot Botkin are hoping to get to us first. I suspect they're watching your apartment, maybe your family, combing Atlanta looking for us.

"We can call the Atlanta P.D.," he added, "and we might even convince them to believe that there was a shooting during the gallery showing Friday night, and that we had nothing to do with it. But we have no evidence that Willfort was involved, unless we find those paintings still in his possession."

"We don't actually know Willfort *was* involved," she couldn't help pointing out.

Something in Blake's expression told her he'd learned more than he'd admitted during his morning out. "What is it?" she demanded. "What do you know?"

"I know that your water is boiling," he said, glancing away from her. "Better get the pasta on. I'll go wash up."

"Blake..."

But he'd already left the room.

"Don't you just want to strangle him sometimes?" Stephanie asked sympathetically.

Resisting an impulse to chase after Blake and make him tell her everything he'd done and heard since he'd left her that morning, Tara turned reluctantly to the other woman. "Yes," she agreed grimly. "I do."

Stephanie's eyes were speculative as they rested for a moment on Tara's face. And then she brightly changed the subject, chattering about inconsequentials while they finished preparing the meal.

"THIS IS CRAZY. It will never work."

Stephanie only smiled in response to Tara's plaintive complaint. "Trust me, Tara. No one will recognize you when I'm finished with you. Now lean your head back over the sink so I can rinse your hair."

Since Blake had convinced her to help them, Stephanie had become quite enthusiastic about the project. Tara didn't want to question the other woman's motives, but she still worried what she was going to look like when Stephanie finished with her.

Tara couldn't help liking Stephanie. She was friendly and amusing and intelligent, and had been so generous with her apartment and her possessions. It was obvious that there was a very close bond between Stephanie and Blake, but Tara was beginning to question her earlier suspicions that the two were lovers. Would Stephanie really be so unquestioningly accepting of Tara's presence if she was in love with Blake?

Stephanie refused to let Tara look in a mirror. "You'll see it when I'm finished," she said airily. And then she pulled out a pair of scissors.

Tara bit her lip. "Um—Stephanie..."

"Trust me," Stephanie said, sounding too much like Blake for Tara's peace of mind. "I know what I'm doing."

"This isn't going to work," Tara said flatly. "You won't be able to make me look so different that the men who've been looking for us won't recognize me."

"Don't bet on it," Stephanie advised, and took the first snip from Tara's hair.

"Even if you can change my appearance, I know absolutely nothing about being a magician's assistant." That was one career Tara had never even considered!

"I've been working with Jeremy Kane on and off for the past ten years," Stephanie said firmly. "I'll help you. And Jeremy will make sure you look like you know what you're doing. He's brilliant."

"But..." A spray of snipped hair fell into Tara's face.

"You'd better close your mouth before you get hair in it," Stephanie suggested cheerfully. "Stop fretting, Tara. You'll do fine."

Nearly an hour later, Stephanie helped Tara into a slinky black dress that closely skimmed Tara's curves and ended in a swirl of skirt at her calves. Stephanie had curled and fluffed Tara's hair and painted her face, but still hadn't allowed her to look in a mirror. She wanted Tara to see "the whole package," she'd said.

Stephanie finally stopped fussing over Tara and stepped back to look her over closely. Tara felt like a department-store mannequin as Stephanie walked slowly around her, studying her from every angle. And then Stephanie stopped in front of her, smiling brightly.

"Perfect," she pronounced. "Ready to take a look?"

Suddenly nervous, Tara cleared her throat. "I'm not sure."

"Didn't I tell you to trust me?" Stephanie took firm

hold of Tara's shoulders and turned her toward the full-length mirror. "What do you think?"

"I think," Tara said, her voice faint, "that there's a stranger hiding in your mirror."

The woman reflected couldn't possibly be Tara. This woman had dark copper hair that curled flirtatiously around her face. As for the face itself—well, suffice it to say that Stephanie was an artist with a makeup brush, Tara thought in wonder. Her usually unspectacular blue eyes had been shaped and shadowed so that they looked huge, with a seductive tilt to the outside corners. Blusher sculpted her cheekbones, making them look more prominent. Her mouth had been outlined with bold, smudge-proof lipstick into a deep crimson pout.

The amount of skin revealed by the low-cut, sleeveless black dress would have made Tara's mother gasp in shock and her father snatch a blanket to wrap around her. Tara hadn't even realized she *had* cleavage until Stephanie had poured her into this dress.

"You," Stephanie said proudly, "are gorgeous."

"You're right," Tara replied blankly. "I am." And how on earth had *that* happened to ordinary Tara McBride?

Stephanie laughed. "Wait until Blake sees you. He already thinks you're beautiful. But seeing you like this is going to knock the socks right off him."

Tara's cheeks flamed beneath the paint. "Stephanie, Blake and I aren't... I mean, we hardly know each other. We've only been thrown together temporarily by circumstances."

Stephanie gave a delicate snort. "I've seen the way

Blake looks at you, Tara. There's more between you than 'circumstances.'"

Tara's cheeks darkened even more as she thought of the kisses she and Blake had shared that very morning—in Stephanie's bed.

Stephanie laughed again. "I knew it," she said in apparent delight. "There is something going on! Oh, I love seeing Blake all shaken up for a change. It's good for him."

Totally bewildered, Tara turned away from the mirror. "Not that there's anything between Blake and me, but…it really wouldn't bother you if there was? You and he aren't…?"

Stephanie sighed heavily. "Honestly, sometimes I just want to strangle him. Tara, Blake is my brother."

Tara felt her jaw drop. "Your…?"

"Brother," Stephanie repeated clearly. "He's five years older than I am. He raised me after our parents died when I was ten and he was barely fifteen."

Tara shook her head. "I didn't know. He didn't tell me."

"We don't tell many people. Ever since I accidentally got involved in one of Blake's cases a long time ago, and almost got myself kidnapped by a guy who thought he could use me to keep Blake from going public with some damaging information, Blake has this crazy idea that it's safer for me if no one knows he has a sister. He should have told you the truth. I don't know why he hasn't, but I refuse to lie to you. I like you."

The touch of defiance in Stephanie's voice might have been amusing, had Tara not still been completely staggered by her admission. "Your brother," she repeated, mentally reassessing everything that had happened since she and Blake had arrived in Savannah.

Blake had to know what she'd been thinking, Tara decided with a sudden flare of anger. He must have realized that she would misinterpret his having a key to Stephanie's apartment. And he'd let her go on thinking that way, even after he'd kissed her until she had been almost ready to throw all common sense to the wind. He'd left her feeling guilty and confused, and had made it very awkward for her when Stephanie had arrived, acting so friendly and welcoming.

Tara thought she just might strangle him herself.

Tara searched the other woman's face for signs of a family resemblance. They were there, just faintly, now that she knew what to look for.

Why on earth hadn't Blake told her the truth?

Stephanie touched Tara's hand. "I know it's none of my business, whatever is going on between the two of you. But...well, Blake has been alone for a long time. He hasn't seemed to truly belong anywhere, and that has bothered me. I've hoped he would find someone nice like you. I love him very much, and I want him to be happy."

"I know you do," Tara replied, her stomach suddenly knotting. "But please don't start matchmaking. This really isn't a good time."

Nor did she have any reason to believe that she was the one who could make Blake happy, she could have added. Tara and Blake were so different. Besides, who knew what would happen when this all ended?

"First you have to make sure you're both safe. I understand. But that doesn't mean I can't have hope for afterward," Stephanie added impishly. Even though she and Stephanie were the same age, Tara thought the other woman seemed much younger at that moment.

"I have to go now," Stephanie said before Tara could argue further. "So you and my brother will be all alone tonight. All night."

Tara rolled her eyes. "Stephanie!"

Stephanie grinned. "Just thought I would point that out. And you really do look beautiful, by the way. You'll make Blake's head spin...and it will be good for him. If I were you, I'd make him sweat a little as punishment for lying to you."

"He didn't actually lie," Tara murmured.

"He didn't tell the truth, either."

"No." And he'd led her to believe he would keep her informed all the way, Tara remembered irritably. Yet he'd told her almost nothing since they'd arrived in Savannah.

She was getting angrier all the time. It would serve him right if she did make him sweat. Unfortunately, Tara had never developed the skills required to turn a man to jelly.

The woman in the mirror, however...

She eyed her reflection thoughtfully as Stephanie slipped quietly out of the room.

9

STEPHANIE MUST not have lingered long after leaving the bedroom she'd offered Tara. It was only a few minutes later when Tara heard someone step through the doorway behind her. She turned slowly from her fascinated contemplation of the striking woman in the full-length mirror—a woman who looked so very different from serious, straitlaced Tara McBride.

Blake had been smiling as he entered the room. When Tara turned to face him, he stumbled to a halt, his smile slowly fading.

In fascination, Tara studied the stunned expression on his face—an expression she'd sometimes witnessed when men first noticed her beautiful cousin, Savannah. Tara didn't remember any man ever looking at *her* quite this way.

The surge of recklessness that poured through her was new to her—and strangely exhilarating.

Blake's gaze traveled slowly from her sexily tousled red curls to her pouty crimson mouth, and then moved downward to take in the shocking dip of her neckline. She wore no shoes, only very sheer black stockings. Holding her head high, she resisted an urge to curl her toes into the carpet like an embarrassed kid.

Blake seemed to grope for words. "Wow," was all he finally said.

Power. She felt her power in the dazed look in his eyes, in the husky edge to his voice.

She'd been able to intimidate men in the past with her intelligence, her determination, her ambition and her position. But she'd never felt the sheer, feminine power of knowing a man had just looked at her and had his knees go weak in response. Never.

And it felt wonderful. Especially with this particular man, who'd already made Tara's knees melt on numerous occasions with his sexy smiles and cocky walk.

"Well? What do you think?" She deliberately lowered her voice an octave as she spoke, holding out her arms and making a slow pirouette. "Will anyone recognize me?"

"I hardly recognize you myself," Blake replied, his voice still sounding a bit odd.

She reached up to run a hand through her newly shortened and curled hair, fully aware that the movement pulled her dress tight against her breasts. "Is that good or bad?"

She watched as Blake's eyes glazed. "I—er—haven't decided."

He took a few steps closer. "I've always thought you were beautiful, Tara. But you look downright deadly now."

She pursed her lips. "I'm not sure that sounds like a compliment."

His gaze focused on her pouting mouth. "I'm not sure I meant it as one."

She reached up to run a fingertip across his lower lip. "Careful, Blake," she warned softly. "The way you're looking at me might just give me ideas."

He slid his hands around her waist. "You've already given me a few," he muttered, pulling her closer.

Feeling daring and wicked and still more than a little annoyed with him, she slid her hands up his chest to his shoulders, her face tilted invitingly upward. "Anything you want to share?"

"Oh, yeah." He ducked his head, and brushed his lips across hers. Once, and then again. She didn't respond, but didn't draw back, either.

"Tara." His voice came out a groan. "You're driving me crazy. I'm trying to keep a clear head, but I can't seem to think straight when you're around. That hasn't happened to me before, especially not in the middle of a case."

His words—and the uncharacteristically humble tone in which he spoke them—jolted her. She steeled herself against the smoldering look in his eyes, reminding herself that he'd lied to her, at least by omission, about Stephanie. He'd let her worry and stew about the other woman, feeling guilty for kissing him in Stephanie's bed, when for all Tara had known, Blake had occupied that bed many times before.

He deserved to suffer, at least a little, for what he'd put her through, she decided.

She rose on stockinged tiptoes to brush a kiss across his mouth. She allowed the very tip of her tongue to trace his lower lip, and, oh, he tasted good. With satisfaction, she felt a tremor of response ripple through him. Placing his hands on her hips, he pulled her closer, letting her know that she'd aroused him.

"Blake." Her lips moved lightly against his. "We really shouldn't do this."

He buried one hand in the soft curls at the back of her head, tilting her face into position for a long, deep kiss. She clung to him, wondering which of them was really being seduced.

Very slowly, he broke the kiss, his lips clinging to hers for just a moment before he spoke. "You're probably right."

But then he kissed her again. And she could almost feel the balance of power shifting in his favor.

His left hand still buried in her hair, Blake slid his right to the small of her back, and then lower, to cup her bottom and pull her more snugly against him. She ached fiercely at every point where their bodies met. If she was going to stop this, she thought, now was the time.

But it wasn't going to be easy.

She braced her hands against his shoulders and pushed, putting a full two inches between them. "We have to stop," she said, though what she really wanted to do was to drag him to the bed and throw all caution to the wind.

She wanted him, as she had never wanted anyone before. But there was still just enough sense of self-preservation inside her to remind her how badly he could hurt her. He had already hurt her by deceiving her about Stephanie after promising not to keep anything from her. No matter what his excuse might be, she felt betrayed by that omission.

Blake tried to pull her back into his arms. "Tara..."

"No, Blake. We can't."

"I'll admit our timing isn't the greatest, but..."

"No," she said firmly. "I can't do this to Stephanie. She's been too nice to me."

He was visibly confused. "Stephanie?"

Gaining confidence, Tara moved another inch backward, so that she wouldn't be rattled by his nearness. "After all she's done for me, I refuse to hurt her by getting involved with you behind her back. It's obvious that she loves you."

Blake winced. "Uh, Tara..."

She smoothed damp palms down her sides, knowing that the movement pressed the dress more tightly against her. "Do you deny that she loves you?" she challenged him, holding his gaze with her own.

She had him there. "No," he admitted, "but..."

She nodded. "I thought so. You should be ashamed, Blake, making passes at me while staying under the roof of a woman you've been stringing along."

"Tara, you don't understand. It isn't like that."

Getting fully into her role, she tossed her head. "I suppose you're going to tell me that you don't love her."

"No. I mean, of course I do, but..."

She was rather enjoying watching Blake squirm. It was the first time since she'd known him that she'd seen him truly rattled. Which was only fair, considering how many times he'd reduced her to near incoherence.

"So you do love her." She sighed soulfully, hoping she wasn't overplaying.

"Yes. Damn it, Tara, she's my sister."

She gasped and placed a hand over her heart, strategically placed to make the most of her newly discovered cleavage. "Your *sister*?"

"Yeah." He had the grace to look penitent. "I suppose I should have told you sooner."

"I would say so," she answered indignantly. "How could you let me go on believing that Stephanie's heart was going to be broken? You cad. You deceiver. You...you..."

"You already knew, didn't you?"

The wry resignation in Blake's voice made Tara choke on a sudden urge to laugh, an urge that faded quickly as genuine anger bubbled up again.

"Stephanie told me the truth," she said coolly. "Unlike you, she didn't think I deserved to be kept in the dark. Why didn't you tell me, Blake?"

BLAKE SAW the angry accusation in Tara's eyes, and he bit back a sigh. He had known Tara would find out the truth about Stephanie eventually, and he'd also known she would be annoyed that he hadn't told her from the beginning.

Actually, he thought, warily studying her expression, "annoyed" didn't quite describe her reaction. Beneath her cool sarcasm, she was furious.

He didn't quite know how to explain his reasons for misleading her. He could tell her it was force of habit, that he'd been protecting Stephanie from the less pleasant aspects of his chosen career for a long time. But that didn't apply here; Tara posed no threat to Blake's little sister.

He could tell her he'd hidden behind Stephanie because he'd been so determined not to take advantage of

Tara's current dependence on him, and hadn't quite trusted his own willpower where Tara was concerned. But that wasn't the whole story, either.

What he didn't know how to explain to her was his reluctance to allow her to get too close. Already she was becoming too important to him. It was getting harder all the time to keep this in perspective, to remind himself that there was no future for them. How could there be, considering the way he'd been living for the past ten years? Never in one place more than a few days at a time, always available at a moment's notice to drop everything and embark on a new adventure, no strings, no ties, no permanent home.

Hell, he rarely even used his full name. As far as he knew, Tara didn't even know it.

Stephanie had seemed like a convenient cover, at least until he got himself under control where Tara was concerned. Maybe he'd had a foolish idea that the less Tara knew about him, the easier it would be for him to keep his emotional distance from her. It hadn't been working.

Tara McBride had gotten under his skin the first time he'd met her, nearly two years ago. Though he'd talked with her only a dozen times at most since that first meeting, he'd never been able to put her completely out of his mind. He was beginning to suspect now that he never would.

"I'm sorry," he said simply, deciding that no explanation could justify his deceiving her. "I should have told you."

"Yes," she answered quietly. "You should have."

She half turned away from him, crossing her arms

over her intriguingly revealed chest. The suddenly defensive gesture told him more than she'd probably intended. He'd hurt her, he realized hollowly. It was the one thing he'd been determined from the beginning not to do.

Even as he struggled with the guilt that realization caused him, a part of him wondered if she would really be so hurt if she hadn't begun to care for him, at least a little.

But, no. That possibility shouldn't please him, he reminded himself. He still had little to offer her, nothing at all compared to the powerful career she'd made for herself long before he'd met her. Sure, she'd hit a wall at the moment, but he had no doubt that she would find a way around it, and with no help from him. Tara was smart, capable, intimidating when she wanted to be. He'd seen her in her office, noted the respect she'd earned from her associates. One setback, no matter how devastating it seemed at the moment, wouldn't hold her down for long.

Maybe she thought she needed Blake now, but that wouldn't last long.

And then who would be hurt?

"What else haven't you told me about our situation?" she asked over her shoulder, refusing to meet his eyes.

"Nothing important," he assured her. "I talked to Jeremy Kane this morning, after I saw the notice that he was going to do the charity thing at Willfort's estate. Jeremy has agreed to help us get in."

"I know why you want in. You want to check Willfort's art collections for the allegedly stolen paintings. I assume you have descriptions of them?"

"Better than that. I have photographs. I had my friend in the insurance company fax them to me at a copy shop this morning."

She nodded, apparently unimpressed. "So that explains why you want to go in, though I can't imagine how you're going to get past Willfort's security and wander through his home at will."

"I'll manage."

"I'm sure you will," she said with a cool, matter-of-fact shrug. "My question is, why do you need me? Why should I pretend to be one of Jeremy Kane's assistants?"

"Because you're the only one who saw the face of the man who grabbed you in that office. I only saw him from behind. I might recognize him again, but I couldn't be sure without you. If he's at Willfort's charity benefit Friday night, I want to know it. I need you to point him out to me."

He watched her throat move as she swallowed hard. He knew she was worried, but she was making every effort to hide her fear. And he admired her more because of it.

"Won't he recognize me?" she asked, her voice only a bit huskier than usual.

Blake studied her new look—the copper curls, the uptilted eyes, her pouting red mouth and seductive black dress. As stunningly beautiful as she looked this way, he was still partial to the Tara he'd always known.

"He won't recognize you," he assured her.

She turned back to the mirror. "I do look different," she murmured.

"You look fantastic," he assured her, taking a tentative step closer to her. "No more or less beautiful than before, only different."

"I only hope I don't screw up and put you—put us both—in more danger."

Blake reached out to place his hands on her shoulders—her mostly bare shoulders, he couldn't help noticing. "You'll do fine."

"But I don't know what I'm doing." She seemed compelled to try to make him understand. "I haven't had any experience at this. It isn't something I feel qualified to do."

Every word she spoke told him more about her deepest insecurities, and about the doubts that had plagued her since the senior partners at her law firm had cravenly refused to stand behind her. Why was it always so important to Tara to be an overachiever? To never make mistakes? To be fully in control of every situation?

How could he help her understand that being slightly imperfect only made her more human? More appealing, as far as Blake was concerned.

He raised his hands to cup her pretty, worried face. "You can do it," he assured her. "I believe in you, Tara McBride."

She reached up to cover his left hand with her right. "Thank you."

Impulsively, he kissed the tip of her nose. "You're welcome."

He didn't release her. She didn't draw back.

"I'm still mad at you," she murmured, though she didn't look particularly angry. In fact, she was looking at him in a way that made his knees weaken, even as other parts of him grew stronger.

"No, you aren't," he answered, hiding the beginning of a smile.

Her mouth twisted wryly. "Well, I'm trying to be."

It really should be a crime for her to wear this dress, Blake mused as he glanced down, only to find himself admiring the porcelain-pale, inner curves of her breasts. He couldn't help wondering if she wore anything beneath the dress. And he wanted very badly to find out.

He had nothing to offer her, he reminded himself again as she tilted her face a bit closer to his. At least, not for the long term. But for tonight...

Tonight he was willing to give her anything she wanted.

BLAKE'S HANDS were so warm, so strong around her face. Tara felt the calluses on his fingertips, the ridge of a small scar on his palm. But, most intriguingly, she felt the faint tremor that rippled through them when she moved a half step closer to him.

There was a special feminine pleasure to be found in causing a strong man to tremble.

She tried to remember that she was annoyed with him. But at the moment, she couldn't recall quite why. She could think of nothing but how good it felt to be so close to him. To have him looking at her as though he wanted to devour her. The same way she was probably looking at him.

Blake believed in her, as no one else had lately. Even Tara herself.

He thought she was beautiful. He'd said so even before her dramatic makeover. It had been a long time since anyone had called her beautiful. A long time since it had mattered to her.

Blake had only to smile at her—the way he was now—to seduce her. And she was getting tired of fighting him. Tired of fighting herself.

She wanted him.

She'd never wanted anyone else like this, and couldn't imagine that she ever would. There couldn't possibly be another man like Blake.

Experimentally, she rose on stockinged tiptoes to brush a kiss across his mouth. Her eyes remained open. She watched as his darkened.

He wanted her.

The old Tara would have made a prudent retreat at this point. The sensible, logical, cautious—and often lonely—Harvard-educated attorney didn't take foolish chances. She wasn't sure that was true of the new Tara—the one with the copper curls and seductress mouth, the one who had been living on the edge of danger for an entire weekend. The one who could make Blake tremble with a kiss.

This new, more daring Tara wanted to experience life more fully than she had before. Maybe even take a few risks.

She kissed him again.

Blake dropped his hands from her face to haul her so tightly against him that she could hardly breathe. Tara didn't complain. Why would she, when it felt so very good?

There wasn't much of a back to the dress Stephanie had put her into. Tara felt Blake's hands on her bare skin, which only made the rest of her crave his touch. She closed her eyes and sank into his kiss, implicitly telling him that she wasn't going to fight either of them tonight.

Blake kissed her until she was clinging to him, uncertain whether her legs would support her if she let go of him. He drew his head back only enough to murmur, "I promised myself I wouldn't take advantage of you."

"Then let me take advantage of *you*," Tara whispered and pulled his mouth back to hers.

Blake seemed to have no problem with that.

Still deep in the kiss, Tara reached between them to unfasten the top button of Blake's green cotton shirt. And then the second. By the time they came up for air, she had the shirt unbuttoned and pulled from the waistband of his khaki slacks.

She spread her hands over his chest, easing the shirt out of the way. He was beautiful, she thought in avid appreciation. Sleek, strong, slim. She leaned forward to place a fleeting, openmouthed kiss on his chin, and then moved lower, kissing a line from his throat to a spot in the middle of his chest. She felt the muscles quivering beneath his skin, the effort he made to be still and let her explore as much as she liked.

It only took her a moment to unbutton his cuffs and push the shirt off his shoulders. She removed it very slowly, letting her fingertips trail along his biceps as she uncovered them.

Blake swallowed audibly.

Tossing his shirt aside, she slid her arms around his lean waist and pressed close. She touched her tongue to his nipple and felt him shudder in response.

"So much for willpower," Blake muttered.

Moments later, Tara's borrowed, sexy black dress was lying on the floor at her feet. She blushed as she stood in front of him in nothing but a tiny scrap of strapless black bra, bikini panties and thigh-high black stockings. The undergarments were her own, the ones she'd worn beneath the black dinner suit Friday evening. The stockings were a newly opened pair of Stephanie's, who'd pointed out that bare legs hardly matched the sleek, sexy dress.

The next thing Tara knew, she was being lifted in the air, high against Blake's chest. It was the first time in her life she'd been literally swept off her feet, picked up and carried to bed in true romantic fashion. She might have even said at one time that she wouldn't appreciate such a gesture, that she wouldn't want to be carried, that she preferred making her own way to bed.

She would have been wrong. She enjoyed every minute of it.

Blake laid her on the bed, then sat beside her to kick off his shoes. Lying against the pillows, Tara ran a hand up his back, pausing at the thick ridge of puckered skin beneath his left shoulder blade, the scar she'd felt when he'd kissed her that morning.

"This looks serious. How did you get it?" She

wanted to know everything about this man who was so different from anyone she'd known before.

"It's a bullet wound," he replied bluntly as he lifted the right leg of his khaki slacks. "I was shot in the back by a man who was stalking one of my clients."

Tara swallowed a sudden knot in her throat, watching mutely as Blake unstrapped the knife sheath he wore on his right calf and set it aside.

Definitely unlike any man she had ever known before, she thought with a mixture of nervousness and fascination. That must explain why he excited her as no other man had before.

Blake stood and unfastened the button of his slacks, then hesitated as he searched her face intently. "Second thoughts?" he asked.

By way of an answer, she reached up to release the front clasp of the strapless bra. The scrap of fabric landed on the nightstand, partially covering his knife sheath.

Blake nearly fell on his face in his hurry to get out of his clothes. Tara was giggling when he tumbled onto the bed beside her. He smothered her laughter with his mouth.

Blake lowered his head to her breasts, nuzzling gently against her, teasing her with nipping kisses and quick flicks of his tongue. Tara inhaled sharply, the movement pressing her more snugly against him. She buried her fingers in his thick golden hair, whispering his name—the only name she knew for him. "Blake."

He kissed her again, his tongue delving deeply into her mouth. His talented fingers kneaded her breasts, slid down her stomach, then slipped between her legs to stroke the tiny, dampening triangle of black lace. Tara arched into his touch, a gasp escaping her. How could he bring her this close to the edge with only a touch?

Blake surprised her by rolling to his back, pulling her on top of him.

"You're the one taking advantage, remember?" he asked her, his grin both roguish and challenging.

Her eyes widened. She became suddenly aware that she was lying on top of him, wearing nothing but panties and stockings, that he was waiting for her to do something...well, exciting. And Tara McBride simply wasn't an exciting person.

At least, the old Tara McBride hadn't been.

Experimentally, she undulated against him. Her silk-covered legs slid seductively against Blake's bare ones.

She heard his quick intake of breath, and her eyes narrowed again.

Maybe this new Tara McBride wasn't so unexciting, after all.

She kissed his chin. His throat. His chest. And then she slid downward and pressed a damp kiss right next to his navel. His stomach contracted sharply. She felt him grow and swell against her abdomen, proving that her tentative efforts to arouse him were as successful as she'd hoped. She planted another kiss on the tender skin an inch below his navel.

"Um...Tara..." He caught her chin with his right hand, just as she worked up the nerve to ease lower. "It's sort of been a while for me."

She smiled in delight and pulled his hand around to

her mouth, pressing a kiss into his palm. "For me, too," she admitted, though she stopped short of telling him that no one had ever made her ache the way she ached now.

And then, just to prove she could, she ducked away from him to brush her lips across his swollen flesh.

Blake made a sound that was somewhere between a groan and a laugh, and then he hauled her upward. "You do like living dangerously, don't you?" he accused her as his arms closed around her.

She could have told him that she didn't like it at all, but that would have been the old Tara speaking. Blake's mouth covered hers before she could say anything.

The world shrank to this one bed, this one man. Tara didn't think about the past or the future, didn't worry about their differences or their circumstances, no longer feared that she wasn't exciting enough or daring enough. She didn't think at all, but allowed herself to act on sheer instinct. Blake seemed to approve wholeheartedly.

He made love to her until she quivered and cried out each time he touched her, her skin so exquisitely sensitized that she felt that she would leap right out of it if they didn't end this soon. She was vaguely aware when he paused long enough to grope for the pants he'd left lying by the side of the bed. She waited impatiently while he ripped a foil packet open with his teeth. And then she helped him don the contents, her hands more eager than skillful.

Blake stripped away Tara's lacy bikini panties. And then he clutched her thighs, just above the tops of the silk stockings, and entered her with one deep, forceful thrust. Tara nearly came off the bed, arching beneath him with a cry of pleasure, her heels digging into the sheets, her hands going to his hips to hold him even tighter.

The sensations that shot through her were more intense, more powerful than anything she'd ever felt before. Her total lack of control over her emotions, her reactions—even over her own movements—should have caused her concern. She'd always been so very careful to remain in control. But with Blake, it simply didn't matter. Oddly enough—considering everything that had happened lately—she felt safe with him.

And then he moved again, and she willingly surrendered what little sanity she'd retained.

10

IT WAS BLAKE'S TATTOO that reminded Tara of how foolish she'd been to think that anything had changed between them just because she'd given in to the temptation of his beautiful blue eyes and flashing smile.

The tattoo was on the back of his right wrist. Tara spotted it when he reached up to brush a damp strand of hair away from her face. She didn't immediately see what it was, but just knowing it was there was enough to bring her back to reality.

What was she doing? Who was this red-haired woman who lay sprawled in such abandon in another woman's bed, wearing nothing but a pair of black silk stockings? And who was this naked man beside her, who'd shared so little of himself with her, who had turned her life upside down by tapping out "shave and a haircut" on her apartment door? Who had somehow made her fall in love with him, even when she knew from the start that doing so was a mistake?

Pushing that thought to the back of her mind, she took his hand and turned it so that she could study the mark on his wrist. Blake didn't resist.

Her eyebrows lifted. "What is this? A wolf?"

"A fox," he corrected her, his expression a bit sheepish.

She could see it now, a tiny silhouette etched in blue,

a sleek, stylized creature captured in full run. *Crazy like a fox,* she thought. *As wily as a fox.*

"I was just a kid when I got that. Nineteen, maybe. And more than a little drunk," Blake admitted.

"Why a fox?"

He lifted one bare shoulder in a hint of a shrug. "It seemed like a good idea at the time."

"Oh."

He smiled in response to her expression. "You pointed out, yourself, that I'm a bit...weird."

"'Weird' was *your* word," she reminded him. "I think mine was 'odd.'"

She reached out and tugged at the hem of the sheet, covering herself with what she hoped was a casual gesture.

Blake slipped out of the bed. "I'll be right back."

He disappeared into the bathroom. Tara immediately stripped out of the thigh-high stockings and reached for the ice-blue satin bathrobe Stephanie had given her to wear earlier, during their hairstyling and makeup session. She felt somewhat more self-possessed now that she was covered. She tied the sash tightly around her waist.

She heard water running in the bathroom, and suddenly she needed to get away from the wildly rumpled bed, the heedless scattered clothing, the man who would, at any moment, walk naked out of that bathroom door. She made a hasty exit from the bedroom, telling herself that she wasn't really retreating—she simply needed something to drink.

Rummaging in Stephanie's refrigerator, she found orange juice, tomato juice, grapefruit juice, canned sodas and designer water. She took out a soda, filled a glass with ice and poured the drink carefully, giving more concentration than necessary to the relatively simple task. She took a sip, feeling the bite of carbonated caffeine, and then she turned toward the doorway.

Blake stood there watching her, wearing nothing but his khaki slacks, his arms crossed over his bare chest as he leaned against the doorway, looking as though he'd been there a while. His golden hair was rumpled around his face, and she couldn't help remembering how thick and luxuriant it had felt when she'd buried her fingers in it.

Since he seemed to be waiting for her to say something, she lifted the glass. "I was thirsty."

He nodded. "I'm a little thirsty, myself."

"What would you like?" she asked politely, taking a half step toward the refrigerator.

He shook his head and pushed away from the door. "I'll get it."

He pulled a can from the refrigerator, popped the top and tilted it to his lips without bothering with a glass. Watching his throat work, and noting the way the light gleamed on his bare chest, Tara felt her mouth go dry again.

Blake was undoubtedly the most beautiful man she'd ever known. She wasn't sure she'd ever be able to look at him without wanting to touch him.

His eyes met hers, and she wondered if he could read her thoughts. But all he asked was, "Having regrets?"

She shook her head. "No. I wasn't carried away by

impulse, Blake. I knew what I was doing. What I wanted. And I have no regrets. Only—"

"Only what?"

"A lot of unanswered questions."

He looked away from her. His gesture told her a great deal.

"You aren't ready to answer them, are you?"

Blake ran a hand through his hair. "If you ask them, I'll answer."

He seemed to brace himself, apparently preparing to bare his soul one question at a time.

Tara had no intention of dragging anything out of him. Not his past, not his feelings, not even his last name. Unless he shared himself with her willingly, there was little point in it. "There's only one question I want to ask now."

He seemed a bit surprised, but he nodded. "All right."

"Why did you come to my apartment Friday afternoon?"

"Because I've wanted you from the first time I saw you," he answered gruffly. "Because when I found out you were no longer with the law firm, I was afraid you would leave town without giving me a chance to see you. Because, no matter how much I told myself I should, I couldn't stay away from you."

Thoroughly shaken by his words, Tara cleared her throat and tried to think of something to say. It was just as well she'd limited herself to one question for now, she thought dazedly. She wasn't sure she could handle any more answers like that one!

Blake gave a rough laugh and set his soda can on the counter. "Sorry you asked?"

Tara put her glass on the table. If she didn't know better, she mused, she would think that Blake's confidence was as precarious as her own in some areas. "I told you," she said, finding her voice again, "I'm not sorry about anything that has happened between us."

Blake reached out and snagged a hand around the back of her neck, pulling her toward him for a long, thorough kiss.

"When this is over—when you're safe—we'll talk," he promised, his lips moving against hers.

She pressed her lips to his again, then drew back far enough to ask, "What are we going to do tonight?"

"Are you hungry?"

"No."

"Neither am I." He kissed her again. "Want to watch TV?"

She slid her arms around his neck, feeling the warmth of his skin through the thin satin robe that was all she wore. "No."

"I suppose we could play poker."

She smiled against his lips. "I don't have any money."

His arms went around her waist. "I suppose strip poker would be a waste of time, considering how little we're wearing."

"I suppose you're right." She wondered how she could want him again so much, so soon.

Funny, she'd never considered herself a particularly passionate woman before. Sex had simply never inter-

ested her all that much. But that had been before Blake
had shown her what she'd been missing.

She pressed closer against him, satisfying herself
that she wasn't the only one who was aroused.
"Blake?"

He nuzzled against her temple. "Mmm?"

"Let's go back to bed."

For the second time that evening—the second time
ever for her—she found herself swung off her feet and
into a man's arms. And, as his muscles rippled beneath
her hands, his arms supporting her as solidly as steel
bars, she found that she liked it every bit as much as
she had before.

TARA WAS MORE than a bit nervous at the thought of
meeting Jeremy Kane. Refusing to raid Stephanie's
closet again, she dressed in her own freshly washed
jeans and aqua-striped T-shirt, sliding her feet into the
inexpensive canvas sneakers Blake had bought to go
with the casual outfit. She styled her hair the same way
Stephanie had the day before, resulting in a cap of friv-
olous copper curls. And she lingered over her makeup,
again copying Stephanie's efforts. When she was finished, she was relatively certain that few of her friends,
or even her family, would have immediately recognized her.

"I can't get over how different you look," Blake said,
sparing her a quick glance when she appeared in the
kitchen.

He'd been amusing himself while he waited for her
by juggling. Tara smiled as she watched five apples

from a bowl on Stephanie's counter dance in the air in front of him. "That's pretty impressive."

His grin was roguish. "I've been told I have very talented hands."

"And I have your fingerprints all over my body to prove it," Tara responded in a contented purr, slowly running her palms down her sides.

To Tara's utter delight, Blake fumbled, and two of the apples crashed to the floor. He managed to catch the other three, though not particularly gracefully. "That," he told her, "was unfair."

She laughed. "Do I smell coffee?"

"It's in the pot. Help yourself." He knelt to retrieve the fallen fruit, still looking a bit disconcerted that she'd managed to rattle him.

Feeling quite pleased with herself, Tara reached for a coffee cup.

After breakfast, Blake drove Tara to an old theater a few blocks from the City Market in the heart of Savannah's restored historic district. He explained that Jeremy had managed to procure the currently idle theater for his rehearsals that week.

He tapped on the back-alley door, which opened almost immediately. Tara looked up at the face of the very large man who stood there, wearing a stretched-to-the-limit black T-shirt with Jeremy Kane's name emblazoned in fancy letters across a massive chest. The man looked fiercely intimidating—until he spotted Blake and smiled.

"Hey, Blake."

"Hey, Pete. This is Tara."

"Ma'am." Pete extended a hand the size of a dinner

plate. It completely swallowed Tara's when she placed hers tentatively into it.

Pete pumped her hand solemnly, then released her and took a step backward. "Jeremy's waiting for you."

He turned to lead them past a bewildering display of props and sets and out onto a stage on which a dark-haired man and two beautiful red-haired women stood looking at a refrigerator-sized steel cage. The man turned around when they entered. Tara's breath caught in her throat.

Jeremy Kane. She'd been an admirer of the famous illusionist since she'd watched his first television special back home in Honoria.

He was still a spectacular-looking man, she couldn't help noticing as he approached. He was in his early forties, his raven-black hair touched with silver at the temples. His eyes were so dark blue they were almost navy, and his smile was as dazzling and magical as his internationally famous performances.

"You must be Tara," he murmured in a deep voice she'd heard only through television speakers before. He took her hand in his.

Momentarily starstruck, she returned his smile. "Yes. And you're Jeremy Kane. I've been a fan of yours since I was a teenager."

And then, realizing how her words had sounded, she blushed and stammered, "Not that you're that much older than I am, of course. I mean, you were very young yourself when you got started."

Still holding her hand, Jeremy laughed. "I assure you, I took no offense. It's always a pleasure for me to meet someone who enjoys my work."

Blake cleared his throat and managed somehow to insert himself between Jeremy and Tara, breaking off their handshake. "How's the family, Jer?"

Jeremy's expression was openly speculative as he looked from Blake to Tara and back again. "Gwen and the children are quite well, thank you. They'll be joining me on tour late next week, when school lets out for the summer."

"How old are the kids now?"

"Harry is six and Beatrice just turned four. Would you like to see a recent photograph?"

"I would," Tara said.

Jeremy smiled, waved his fingers, and magically produced a wallet-sized photograph, which he gravely offered to her. She couldn't help wondering if he always kept it up his sleeve, or wherever it was he'd produced it from.

Smiling in delight at the illusion, she looked at the photograph of Jeremy's family. Though Jeremy was known for surrounding himself with gorgeous redheads in his act, the woman he'd married had brown hair, a face that was more pretty than classically beautiful, and a smile that looked serene and perhaps a bit shy. The children had inherited their father's more striking looks, both of them having his dark hair and dark blue eyes. The mischief in the boy's face and the echoing glimmer in his little sister's beaming smile made Tara suspect that Jeremy's wife had her hands full.

"A very nice-looking family," Tara said as she returned the photograph.

Jeremy looked at it for a moment with love and pride

visible in his expression, and then his fingers waved and the photograph vanished. "Perhaps you'll meet them someday. You would like my wife, I think."

"I'm sure I would."

"Jeremy." A heavily pregnant, auburn-haired woman who might have been a year or two older than Tara appeared from backstage and approached them with a cellular telephone in her hand. "I'm sorry to interrupt, but you need to take this call. It's Mortie."

Jeremy nodded. "Noelle, you know Blake, of course, and this is his friend, Tara. Noelle is my personal assistant," he added by way of explanation for Tara's benefit. "Now, if you'll excuse me, I'll try to make this quick."

Blake looked at his watch as Jeremy moved away. "Stephanie should be here soon to help you learn what Jeremy wants you to do in the act," he told Tara. "I have to leave now. I'm meeting someone."

"We'll take good care of her, Blake," Noelle said in her musical voice. "Tara, let me introduce you to Paula and Monica, who are working as Jeremy's stage assistants on this tour."

Tara hesitated, looking at Blake. "You'll be careful?"

He leaned over to kiss her, not seeming to care whether anyone was watching. "I'll be careful," he promised. "Have fun, sweetheart. But not too much," he added with a ferocious scowl in Jeremy's direction.

Noelle tucked her hand companionably beneath Tara's arm. "My, my," she murmured, sounding quite amused as she looked in the direction in which Blake had disappeared. "I've known Blake for a long time, and I was beginning to think I would never see that look in his eyes."

"Er—what look?"

"The one I saw when you were smiling at Jeremy," Noelle replied with a chuckle. "Blake has most definitely taken the fall—and it's about time."

WHEN BLAKE walked back into the theater a few hours later, he found that Tara had been cut neatly in half. Her head was laughing inside a box while her feet wiggled furiously in another box some seven feet away.

"Jeremy," Blake said with a heavy sigh. "Why is it that every time I leave someone in your safekeeping, you feel compelled to slice'n'dice them?"

Tara giggled, turning her apparently severed head to smile broadly in Blake's direction. "Look at me, Blake. I'm doing magic!"

"Well, to be more precise, you're having magic done to you," Blake said with a chuckle. "You were planning to put her back together, weren't you, Jer?"

Jeremy smiled. "I think that can be arranged."

He waved his hand and Paula and Monica, the two redheads currently on tour with him, efficiently brought the two halves of the box back together. With a few dramatic gestures and ceremonies, they lifted the lid and Tara popped out.

"Arms up, Tara," Jeremy prompted. "The way I showed you before."

Her arms lifted obediently, spread into a posture that invited enthusiastic applause. Blake obliged.

Stephanie appeared suspiciously soon afterward,

her red hair a bit mussed. Blake murmured, "I thought Tara's feet had suddenly grown bigger."

Stephanie punched his arm. "Where have you been?"

"Busy." Blake draped an arm around Tara's shoulders, unable to resist brushing a quick kiss across her flushed cheek. "Having a good time?"

"It's been fascinating," she admitted. "I had no idea how much work went into setting up these performances. Jeremy has let me see a few of his illusions up close, and I've given my word that I'll never reveal anything I've learned."

"Under penalty of permanent dismemberment," Jeremy added congenially. He looked at Blake. "She's going to do great."

"Didn't I tell you she would?"

"What about you? Have a productive day?"

Blake rubbed the back of his neck. "Not as much as I would have liked."

"Sorry to hear that. Anything I can do?"

Blake shook his head. "You're doing enough. Thanks."

One of the young redheads tapped Jeremy's arm. "Paula and I are going to do some sight-seeing if we're finished for the day. Stephanie's been telling us about some of the cool spots in Savannah, and we'd like to go check them out."

Jeremy nodded. "Have a good time. But be careful."

She rose to kiss his cheek, much as she would have if he were her overprotective big brother—the way most of Jeremy's assistants seemed to view him, Blake had always thought. "See you later, boss."

Jeremy turned to Noelle. "What are your plans for the evening?"

She smiled and patted her protruding tummy. "Junior and I are going to get some rest. And I promised Jeff I'd call him."

Jeremy turned to Stephanie. "Steph?"

"Hot date," she answered with an apologetic smile.

Jeremy heaved an enormous sigh and looked soulfully at Blake and Tara.

Blake couldn't help grinning at his friend's hangdog expression. "Would you like to join us for dinner tonight?"

Jeremy grinned. "I'd love to. Thanks."

Blake was almost glad Jeremy would be joining them that evening. He'd spent the whole day replaying the night he and Tara had spent together, and the emotions that lingered inside him had almost overwhelmed him at times. He didn't want to put a name to what he felt for her; he superstitiously imagined that calling it by name would give it that much more power over him. But deep inside, he knew the truth. And it scared him spitless.

He glanced at Tara, to find her smiling a bit too warmly at Jeremy. "We would love to have you join us," she said. "I want to hear all about your career. You've led such a fascinating life."

Blake felt a frown draw his eyebrows downward. Maybe having Jeremy along for the evening wasn't such a great idea, after all. He'd had no idea that Tara was such a fan of the guy. She'd almost hyperventilated when he'd introduced them.

And he was a certifiable idiot for standing here stewing in jealousy just because she was smiling at another man.

"Let's get out of here," he said a bit more gruffly than he'd intended. "I'm hungry."

"Oh, is that what you are?" Jeremy asked in a murmur meant for Blake's ears alone.

Blake gave his friend a warning glare that didn't seem to intimidate the other man at all.

"TELL ME how long you two have known each other," Tara said over dinner in a quiet little seafood restaurant not far from the busy harbor area. "How did you meet?"

She watched as Blake and Jeremy exchanged a quick glance. Jeremy seemed to be silently asking just how much Blake wanted to tell her; Blake looked as though he was trying to decide. And Tara felt a pang at this reminder that there was so much about Blake that was still a mystery to her, so many things that Stephanie and Jeremy and Noelle knew that Tara did not.

"I've known Jeremy since I was just a kid," Blake finally replied. "He was just getting started, working as an apprentice for an illusionist named Renaldo Ciccione. Renaldo was a friend of my father's."

"I taught Blake how to juggle," Jeremy boasted.

"My mother taught me how to juggle," Blake corrected him. "You merely improved on my technique."

There were many more questions Tara wanted to ask. About his parents—what they'd done, how they'd died. About Blake's past—who had taken him in when he'd been orphaned, how he'd ended up as a private investigator.

Blake looked at her, and she knew he saw the questions in her eyes. "Later," he mouthed.

She nodded and turned back to Jeremy. "Tell me more about your wife and children," she suggested, a topic he took up without hesitation.

She was beginning to believe that Blake had invited Jeremy to dinner as much to avoid being alone with her and her questions as to share his friend's company. And his continued reticence hurt, especially considering the night they'd spent in each other's arms.

BLAKE UNLOCKED the door to Stephanie's condo later that evening and then stood aside to allow Tara to go in ahead of him. She seemed to take care not to touch him as she passed. She immediately turned on the overhead lights when she entered, dispelling the romantic glow of the full moon pouring through the glass wall of the living room.

"Stephanie won't be spending the night here?" she asked without looking at him.

"No. She's spending a lot of time with her boyfriend these days. He's a doctor of some sort. I think they're talking marriage."

"Have you met him?"

"Mmm. Nice guy. I think he and Steph will be happy together. She's always wanted kids, and she's not getting any younger. It's time she settled down and quit running all over the world modeling and working with Jeremy."

"She can still work and have children. Jeremy does."

"But Jeremy's wife is content to stay home and take care of their kids when he's out on tour. In fact, she says there's nothing she would rather do. Stephanie's boyfriend works long hours in his medical practice. Someone will have to stay home to raise those kids, and it's probably going to be Stephanie. She told me it's what she wants. She's tired of being on the road."

"And what about you, Blake?" Tara turned to face him then. "Don't you ever want to settle down? Do *you* ever get tired of being on the road?"

He sighed, and this time he was the one who looked away. But he answered honestly. "It's all I've done for so long that it's the only way I know how to live."

"I suppose it's a relatively easy existence. No ties, no commitments, no sticky emotional attachments. You don't even claim your own sister most of the time."

The edge in her voice piqued him. "That's hardly fair. You don't really know enough about my life to judge it."

"No, I don't, do I?" Sounding as though she felt she'd scored another point, Tara turned her back to him. She stood looking out the window at the river beyond, her arms crossed over her chest, her expression distant, pensive.

Remembering how her face had glowed with enthusiasm when he'd rejoined her at the theater earlier, Blake wondered what had abruptly changed her mood. "Tara? Are you upset? Have I said or done something wrong?"

"I'm fine."

"Obviously you aren't." He risked taking a step closer, though something in her stance warned him not to touch her just yet. "What's wrong? You seemed to be having such a good time with Jeremy and his assistants.''

''A good time? Did I seem to be having a good time, Blake?''

He reached out to place his hands on her shoulders, turning her to face him. ''Tell me what's wrong.''

She lifted her chin and looked defiantly at him. ''Two weeks ago, I lost a job I'd been working toward my entire life. A little over seventy-two hours ago, a man died at my feet. Someone tried to shoot us. Someone invaded my apartment. You tell me that we're going to break into the home of one of the most powerful men in the state to find evidence that he has committed insurance fraud, that he might be behind the murder in the gallery. We'll probably be arrested—if, that is, we don't get shot like poor Mr. Botkin. Oh, yes, Blake, I'm having a very good time.''

Guilt crashed through him, nearly prompting him into making rash promises that he had to bite back with an effort. He knew in that moment that he would have offered her anything she wanted—his very life, if necessary.

He loved her. There was no reason to continue to deny it. Calling it by any other name didn't change the truth. He was in love with her, and he had been for quite some time. And look what he had done to her, what he had no choice but to continue to do to her for another few days.

How much more proof did he need that he was all wrong for her?

He tugged her into his arms. She didn't resist, but buried her face in his shoulder for a moment. And then she drew a deep breath and lifted her head. "I'm sorry. I shouldn't take my frustration out on you."

He spoke forcefully, guilt weighing even more heavily on him. "You have no reason to apologize. If it weren't for me, you wouldn't be in this mess."

"No. I would still be sitting in my apartment sulking and staring at the television," she replied with a wan smile.

"You would be safe."

She shook her head. "Blake, no matter what I said, I don't blame you. I suppose I was angry with myself."

"Why?"

She ran a hand through her red-dyed curls, in a weary gesture. "Maybe because I *was* having a good time today. In the theater, at dinner. I suddenly felt...I felt so guilty for enjoying myself after—" She groped ineffectively at the air with her right hand, unable to finish.

"How often do you allow yourself to really have a good time, Tara? And I'm not just talking about the last three days."

She flinched, and he knew he'd struck a nerve. "I know how to enjoy myself," she said, her tone defensive.

"Oh? What are your hobbies?"

"I—" She stopped, biting her lip, then shrugged. "I like to read."

"What else?"

"I work," she answered simply.

"And now that you have no job?" he asked gently. "What will you do with your time?"

Her arms tightened, her hands rubbing her forearms

as though to ward off a sudden chill. "I don't know," she whispered.

He loosened her fingers and tugged her icy hands into his, holding them tightly, sharing some of his warmth with her.

"If there is one thing I've learned during the past twenty years, it's to take your pleasure where you can find it," he said. "The situation we're in is serious, there's no denying that. And what we're planning to do Friday night will not be fun. But there is no reason for you to feel guilty because you enjoyed yourself for a few minutes today."

He lifted her hands to his mouth, kissed one, and then the other. "You've been amazing during the past three days. Don't fall apart on me now. I need you."

Her face softened a bit, but she shook her head. "You don't need anyone. Especially me."

"Now that," he said, leaning over to brush her mouth with his, "is the first really foolish thing you've said all evening."

He kissed her again. And then again. And, finally, she began to respond.

Her hands slipped out of his to go around his neck. She pressed closer. "Blake?"

Already he could feel himself responding to her, aching for her. Maybe he'd believed—maybe he'd even hoped—that making love with her last night would blunt the edge of his desire for her. Maybe he'd thought he could keep his emotions under control once he'd satisfied that first urgent hunger.

He'd been wrong. He wanted her as much now as he

had before. More. Now that he knew just how spectacular it could be.

His hands slid down to her hips, holding her against him. "Mmm?"

Her lips moved against his cheek, her breath warm and arousing against his skin. "What you said about taking pleasure where you can find it..."

He smiled. "Yes?"

"I'd really like to find some now."

"I'd be more than happy to oblige, ma'am," he murmured. "What would you like me to do to entertain you?"

"Well...I suppose you could juggle."

He laughed softly. "I suppose I could."

"Or...you could take me to bed."

He kissed her flushed cheek, and then her mouth. "That would certainly be my choice."

There were still shadows in her eyes, but she was smiling when she drew back to take his hand and walk with him toward the bedroom.

11

SOMETIME during that night, Tara made a decision. It was becoming obvious that Blake wasn't going to open up to her. That he intended to keep his past an enigma. She suspected that there were also things about their current situation that he was keeping from her, things he learned during the mysterious forays he took while leaving her with Stephanie and Jeremy.

Something was going on that he hadn't told her, she realized. Whether he was trying to protect her, or whether he simply didn't trust her, his reasons didn't particularly matter to her. The very fact that he wasn't being entirely honest with her was enough to let her know that any foolish fantasies she might have been harboring about him were just that—impossible day-dreams. It was time to snap out of them. Long past time for her to get a grip on the precarious emotions that had controlled her since she'd lost her job.

She was an attorney. A good one. Though she would probably encounter some awkwardness, she would find another position, and she would make full use of the education she'd worked so hard to attain. Blake had helped her see that, and she was grateful, even if he had come dangerously close to breaking her heart in the process.

All her life, she'd attacked every challenge with determination, intelligence and a refusal to be anything but the best at what she did. It was past time she remembered how to do that, too. She had never in her adult life relied on anyone to take care of her.

As for Blake—well, she could handle him, too. As long as she kept in mind that it ended Friday night, one way or another, she could keep her feelings in perspective. He was the one who'd advised her to take her pleasure where she could find it...and she planned to follow that suggestion.

She would relish the few days they spent together, and then she would put them behind her and move on—Blake's own personal philosophy, she suspected. Tara McBride had always been a quick study. And in the area of guarding her heart, she suspected Blake had quite a bit to teach her.

DURING THE NEXT three days, Blake tried and failed to figure out what was going on in Tara's head.

She'd changed since their talk Monday evening, in ways he couldn't quite define. She seemed more confident, more determined, more self-reliant—more like the woman he'd first met at the law firm. And yet, different. She smiled at Blake's jokes, held up her end of their conversations, went willingly into his arms at the end of each day...but she held back some private, important part of herself, which was becoming increasingly frustrating for him.

Sometimes he looked at this cool, copper-haired, sexily dressed woman and he wondered what she had done with the real Tara McBride. And he wondered a bit wistfully if he would ever have a chance to be with her again.

She was probably going to hate him by the time this was all over. He'd kept too much from her—his past, his relationship with Stephanie, the things about this case that he still hadn't told her. Things she would have to find out, eventually. And she was likely to go for his throat when she learned the truth. She would probably never want to see him again.

Maybe it was for the best. He'd known all along that their time together was only temporary. He wasn't the staying-around type. He was following his usual routine, he thought with grim humor. Rush to the rescue, use whatever means necessary to solve the problem, then quietly fade into the sunset when he was no longer needed. It was a satisfying life, on the whole...but a lonely one.

It was the only life Blake knew. The only one he deserved.

ON FRIDAY EVENING, exactly one week after Blake had shown up on Tara's doorstep, Stephanie stepped back from Tara with a smile of satisfaction. "I've done it again," she bragged. "You look fantastic."

Tara glanced into the full-length dressing-room mirror to see how she looked in the glittering, colorful costume Stephanie had provided for her. "Is it really necessary for these costumes to be so skimpy?"

From the doorway of the dressing room, she heard Blake's voice. "Don't you know why magicians' assistants are traditionally beautiful women in sexy costumes? It's a distraction—so the men in the audience will pay more attention to the women's legs than to the magician's sleight of hand. Makes it less likely they'll figure out the secrets."

Tara turned, and then had to clear her throat. Blake had dressed the part of the stage technician he was pretending to be, wearing faded jeans, a Jeremy Kane T-shirt with the sleeves rolled up on his biceps, and heavy work boots. His hair was tousled more than usual, and a red bandana was tied around his forehead to hold it out of his eyes when he worked. The small tattoo on his right wrist was visible, as was the intriguing scar on his forehead. He looked tough, unpolished, a bit disreputable, far different from the stylishly dressed man who had so often visited the law firm of Carpathy, Dillon and Delacroix.

No matter how he dressed, Tara still thought he was the most spectacular man she'd ever seen.

"And what keeps the women in the audience from watching too closely?" she asked, trying to hide her reaction to him.

"Honey, when Jeremy Kane's on stage, there's not a red-blooded woman alive who can concentrate on his hands," Stephanie quipped. "Especially when he wears those tight black pants."

Tara laughed. "I suppose I can understand that."

Blake gave a disgusted snort. "Would you two like me to leave the room so you can discuss this in more detail?"

Stephanie's grin was wicked. "Not necessary. I'd be perfectly happy to discuss Jeremy's attributes in front of you. Wouldn't you, Tara?"

"Please," Blake cut in. "Spare me."

"I think my brother's feeling insecure, Tara. Maybe you'd better tell him how pretty he is to make him feel better," Stephanie teased, earning a glare from Blake.

"Oh, I think Blake knows well enough how pretty he is," Tara answered lightly.

Stephanie laughed. "Blake, have I mentioned that I really like her?"

Blake had been looking at Tara with a slight frown. He erased it with a smile that seemed a bit forced when he glanced at his sister. "I like her, too."

Stephanie glanced at her watch. "Almost show time. Everyone else is already dressed and waiting backstage. Any last questions, Tara?"

Tara shook her head. "I think I'm ready."

Stephanie looked at Blake again. "Jeremy would love to hire her full-time. He told me she's one of the hardest workers and quickest learners he's ever worked with. I might have gotten my feelings hurt, except that I happened to agree with him."

Tara felt her cheeks warm. "Jeremy's a tough boss," she said lightly. "I don't dare make a mistake."

Stephanie laughed. "He's a major perfectionist when it comes to the act—but that's why he's the best. And under all that tough talk, he's a sweetheart."

Blake scowled. "Saint Jeremy," he muttered.

Grinning, Stephanie patted his cheek. "Jealous?"

"Stuff it, Steph."

Tara tried to smile at their nonsense, ignoring the butterflies that fluttered in her stomach.

They'd driven through the massive gates of Willfort's estate an hour earlier. Blake had come in one of the prop trucks with Jeremy's road crew. Tara had ridden in a limousine with Paula, Monica and Stephanie. Jeremy would arrive in a celebrity limo with some of the other honored guests of the evening.

Jeremy had utterly forbidden Noelle to join them that evening, though Tara had been told Noelle usually coordinated things backstage before a performance. He'd put Stephanie in charge of Noelle's usual tasks.

Stephanie glanced at her watch. "I'd better go check on everything. Blake, you're sure everything's okay?"

"Don't worry. I know what I'm doing."

She kissed his cheek as she passed him on the way out. "Be careful."

"Always."

Stephanie rolled her eyes skeptically, and then left Blake and Tara alone in the dressing room.

Tara turned back to the mirror. Her reflection still startled her. The red hair. The overly dramatic makeup. The costume that was little more than a se-quined bathing suit. Her legs looking longer than usual in dark stockings and spiked heels.

"I look like a tart," she said wryly, trying to imagine her parents' expressions if they could see her like this. Or, worse, her brothers'.

"You look stunning," Blake corrected her. "How are you feeling?"

"A little nervous. Stage fright, I guess."

"Perfectly understandable. But you'll do fine. And, most importantly, you'll be safe with Jeremy."

Tara turned away from the mirror. "Can you believe this place? I've never known anyone who had a theater in his backyard."

"Willfort likes to consider himself a connoisseur of

the arts. He stages summer stock and musical performances here, as well as other charity fund-raisers like this one tonight. He had this theater built about ten years ago."

"He sounds like quite a pillar of society."

"Does he?"

Blake crossed his arms and Tara couldn't help noticing the bulge of muscle beneath the short sleeves of his T-shirt. He usually wore long sleeves, she realized. The loose-fitting clothes he generally preferred camouflaged the sheer strength of his slender body.

Tara, for one, would never underestimate him again.

"Blake." She reached out to place a hand on his arm. "Promise me you'll be careful tonight. I'm worried about you. What if you get caught looking for...well, you know."

"I won't get caught. Don't worry."

"The security guards..."

"One of them works for me."

She blinked, looking up at him in surprise. "For *you?*"

He nodded, his expression grave. "Willfort hired a couple of extra guards to help out with the crowds tonight. One of them reports to me. So I have backup."

"I'm glad to hear that. Um...is there anything else you haven't told me about tonight?"

The look of guilt that flitted across his expression was answer enough. Tara sighed.

"When this is over," Blake said, "we'll talk."

She nodded and drew back. "I'd better hurry. I'm supposed to meet the others backstage."

"Is your lipstick the smudge-proof kind?"

She automatically glanced at the mirror, focusing on her bright crimson mouth. "Yes. Is something wrong with it?"

"No. Just didn't want to mess it up when I did this."

With only that warning, Blake smothered her lips beneath his for a long, thorough kiss. Tara was clinging to him by the time he drew slowly away.

"Tara, I—" He bit off whatever he might have said. "We'll talk later," he promised instead.

She nodded, her voice temporarily gone.

He took a step backward. "C'mon. I'll walk you backstage."

Taking a deep breath for courage, Tara fell in beside him.

SOMETIMES DURING the next hour, Tara found herself fighting the urge to pinch herself to see if she was dreaming. How many tax attorneys had the chance to perform with an internationally famous magician? Jeremy's act was a spectacular one—pounding music, flashing lights, elaborate sets and, of course, his breathtaking illusions.

She saw Blake only once after the performance began, just long enough to whisper to him that she didn't see the big man from the gallery among the enthusiastic audience in Willfort's private little theater. And then Blake disappeared, presumably to execute his own plans for the evening, and Tara went back to work.

She took the performance seriously, giving it her full concentration. She'd only been half joking to Stephanie about being afraid to make a mistake—Jeremy Kane truly was a demanding taskmaster when it came to his work. She identified with that trait well enough not to complain. She'd always been a perfectionist herself when it came to work. It was that determination to have everything done correctly that had made it impossible for her to give in to the senior partners' demand that she knowingly do something she knew was wrong.

She had worked as hard learning this act as she ever had researching a tax question. And it had paid off with Jeremy's praise and her own confidence that she wouldn't make a total fool of herself this evening.

Tara's big act—the one that justified her presence there—came close to the end of the production. She was ceremoniously locked into a large fiberglass ball, which was then rolled playfully around the stage in time to driving rock music. At the end of the number, Jeremy would open the ball, only to reveal to the audience that Tara had been replaced by a beautiful, well-trained Irish setter.

The entire cast—with the exception of Tara, of course—would be on stage for that dramatic unveiling. She would be hiding alone in the wings after slipping from the hidden trap, waiting for her cue to take her bow. She almost looked forward to the thunderous applause she was certain to receive after Jeremy's clever performance.

Hearing the opening notes of the music, she drew a deep breath, pasted on the bright stage smile Stephanie had taught her and stepped onto the stage.

SMUGLY SATISFIED with his own performance that evening—all except for one loose end still left dangling—

Blake slipped into the theater in time to hear the music begin. He recognized it as what he and Tara had called "the big ball number," and he found a spot in the back where he could stand unnoticed to watch.

Tara stepped onto the stage, looking so beautiful his breath caught, smiling in a way that let him know she was enjoying herself. He scanned the audience quickly, realizing with a slight frown that he wasn't the only man who was close to drooling over her. And then he looked back toward the stage.

Jeremy helped Tara climb into the lower half of the colorful ball. At a wave of Jeremy's hand, his other three assistants—Stephanie, Paula and Monica—lifted the top half of the sphere and snapped it into place, completely concealing Tara within it. And then the fun began. The audience laughed as Jeremy and his assistants began to play with the large ball, rolling it around the stage, batting it between them, making everyone believe that Tara was getting quite a workout in there.

Blake heard the amazed gasps when the ball—which had never left the audience's sight—was opened to reveal the Irish setter, who barked and rose on his haunches, begging for the applause he received in spades. Blake knew that Tara was to appear from the wings in a puff of smoke soon afterward to receive her own accolades.

The smoke arrived, but Tara didn't.

Blake saw the slight frown that darkened Jeremy's face as he turned his head to look in the direction from which Tara should have made her entrance. The three women posturing behind him also looked surreptitiously that way, their smiles frozen in place, but just a bit puzzled.

The audience continued to applaud, apparently believing that everything was as it should be.

And Blake was hit with a feeling so strong it almost knocked him backward. Something was wrong with Tara. Seriously wrong.

His heart in his throat, Blake dashed toward the back of the theater.

THE BEEFY HAND that covered Tara's face was ominously familiar. And so was the rough-edged voice that growled in her ear. "Did you really think I wouldn't know you, just because you've changed your hair color? As soon as I spotted your boyfriend, I knew you'd be around somewhere."

He dragged her through the backstage shadows toward the exit. Frantically, Tara wondered where Pete was, or any of Jeremy's other staff.

Blake!

Her captor pushed through the back door, dragging her outside and then pulling her into what might have been a formal garden behind the main house. Tara tried to resist him, fighting him every step of the way, but she was no match for his strength. He held her left arm behind her, the pain so intense that tears leaked from her eyes despite her best efforts to hold them in.

Tara wondered where Willfort's guards were—but then she reminded herself that this man very likely worked for Willfort.

He paused close to a huge magnolia tree, where Tara was quite sure they blended into the shadows. Even her spangled costume wouldn't be visible here, away from the security lights that dotted the estate.

She could hear the man breathing roughly, heavily in her ear—more from anger than exertion, she sensed. Her futile struggles hadn't caused him undue effort.

"We're going to the parking lot on the other side of the theater," he growled. "And you are going to keep quiet, you got that?"

With his hand over her mouth, Tara couldn't have answered if she'd wanted to. She struggled again, her protests muffled against his palm.

"Shut up," he said, jerking at her arm again, hurting her so badly her stomach lurched. "And be still. It's your fault you're here—you and your P.I. boyfriend. Willfort can take the fall for his stupid insurance-fraud plan, but I'll be damned if I'm going down with him. I need money to get out of the country. We'll see if your boyfriend and his rich magician buddy are willing to pay to get you back."

"Let her go, Doren."

Tara almost sagged in relief at the sound of Blake's voice.

The man holding her reacted quite differently. His hold on Tara tightened until she felt her head begin to spin from the pain in her arm and the lack of oxygen. "Back off. I mean it, man, I'll snap her neck. She'll be dead before you take two steps."

Tara had no doubt that he could—and would—do exactly as he said.

The man Blake had called Doren had his back to the magnolia, making sure no one crept up on him from behind. His attention was focused on Blake, who, in his black T-shirt and jeans, was barely visible in the shadow of the tree.

"Don't take another step," Doren ordered. He shoved Tara's twisted arm higher behind her back, making her cry out in pain. The sound was muffled by Doren's hand, but she knew Blake heard it.

"Let her go. It won't do you any good to take her," Blake said, his voice low and unnaturally controlled. "The police know everything. Botkin has already identified you as the man who shot him."

Tara's eyes went wide above Doren's hand. Botkin was alive? Could that possibly be true?

"I'm not going down," Doren insisted, his gravelly voice taking on a desperate edge. "I need money. Travel arrangements. If you want your friend back, you'll help me."

"I can't, Doren. It's too late."

"Then it's too late for *her*." Another vicious twist of Tara's arm brought another cry of pain to her smothered lips. She heard something snap. Stars exploded in front of her eyes, and she was sure for a moment that she would pass out. She fought the weakness with every ounce of her strength.

"No! Damn it, Doren, leave her alone."

A column of bright light suddenly shot up from the ground near Doren's feet, like a sudden eruption of fire from the very ground they stood on. For a moment, Tara thought her pain was making her hallucinate, but Doren flinched back from the leaping flames. He and Tara were spotlighted for an instant in that weird glow, which reflected blindingly from the sequins on Tara's costume. Doren dropped his hand from Tara's face to shield his eyes, taking her out of immediate danger of having him snap her neck.

Trying to ignore the agonizing pain in her arm, she took advantage of the opportunity to escape. She kicked her right foot backward, her spiked heel digging into Doren's shin. As he yelped and instinctively released his hold, Tara shoved herself away from him.

And then something whizzed past her to slam into her captor's shoulder. Doren cursed, and staggered backward. A moment later he went down with two men on top of him—one of them a uniformed security guard, the other Blake.

Tara's left arm fell heavily to her side, useless. She stumbled and would have fallen if someone hadn't caught her.

"Are you all right?" Jeremy asked her, cradling her against him.

Clutching his black dinner jacket with her right hand, she sagged against him, her knees refusing to support her. "The fire," she gasped. "You did that?"

"Seemed like a good idea at the time. I was impressed that you took immediate advantage of the chance to get away from the jerk. Good job, Tara."

Other people were suddenly running toward them. Lights flashed, voices shouted. And Tara felt herself giving in to the agony radiating from her left arm.

Her knees buckled completely. Jeremy supported her, murmuring reassurances.

And then Blake was there.

"Tara." His voice was strangled. "Tara, I'm so sorry."

Jeremy eased her into Blake's familiar arms, saying, "I'll get an ambulance."

Tara opened her mouth to order him to do nothing of the sort. She didn't need an ambulance. It was only a bruised arm, for Pete's sake.

But nothing emerged from her dry, tight throat except a hoarse exclamation of pain.

"She's going into shock, Blake." It was Stephanie's voice that time. "We need to lay her down."

"Blake?" Tara's voice was a bare whisper. She tried to hold onto his shirt as he lowered her gently to the grass.

"Don't try to talk, sweetheart."

He was leaning close to her, but for some reason she was having trouble focusing on his face, even with all the light that had suddenly appeared around them. She struggled to make herself heard over the confusion. "I have to...know. Is Botkin...alive?"

"Yes. He's alive. Thanks to you, Tara. If you hadn't gone into that office when you did, Doren would have finished him off."

The sheer relief of knowing that she hadn't helplessly watched a man die was almost too much for Tara. "Oh, Blake, I..."

"*Shh*. Rest now. We'll talk later."

That suddenly seemed like a very good idea. Tara closed her eyes and let Blake take care of her one more time.

12

"YOUR APARTMENT is very nice."

In response to Stephanie's comment, Tara glanced around the living room that now looked so strange to her, though it had only been eight days since she'd last been in it. "Thank you."

At least Doren, or whoever had been inside her apartment, hadn't made too much of a mess after he'd let himself in with her key, she found herself thinking rather distantly. A few drawers had been riffled through as Doren had looked for clues to where Tara might be hiding, but there'd been no real damage done. The only thing that looked out of place was the dead rose stuck in a crystal bud vase on her coffee table.

Gazing at that rose, Tara felt her heart clench. It seemed almost as if months had passed since Blake had pressed the vivid red bloom into her hand.

Sitting in the wingback chair Blake had occupied that afternoon eight days ago, Stephanie sipped the soft drink Tara had offered her when they'd arrived an hour earlier. "It's a shame Doren wouldn't tell you what he did with your purse," she said. "Now you'll have to replace everything in it."

"There wasn't that much," Tara answered with a shrug that caused a twinge of discomfort in her left arm, which was immobilized in a bulky cast and suspended in a sling. "I'd just stuffed a few things in it for the evening. It won't be that hard for me to replace everything."

"Good." Stephanie looked around the living room again, and cleared her throat. "Is there anything else I can do for you this afternoon? I'd be happy to run to the grocery store. I'm sure you need some supplies."

"No, I have enough for now. But thank you."

Tara shifted to a slightly more comfortable position on her sofa, cradling her injured arm in her lap. The medication she'd taken three hours earlier, prior to the trip from Savannah on a small, private jet Jeremy Kane had generously provided for her, was beginning to wear off. Her arm ached dully in a promise of worse to come.

"Stephanie, I'm so grateful to you for accompanying me on this trip, but there's no need for you to hang around here. I'll probably just get some rest and then make some calls later this afternoon. Jeremy's pilot is waiting for you at the airport, and I know you're ready to get back to Savannah. I'll be fine."

Stephanie bit her lip. "I really hate to leave you here alone."

"I've been living here alone for five years," Tara answered gently.

"Not with a broken arm."

Tara smiled weakly and patted her cast. "It's not exactly a debilitating injury. I'm right-handed. And I have friends I can call if I need anyone. When I talked to my mother this morning and told her everything, she even offered to take a leave of absence from her job and move in with me for a while. It was all I could do to talk her out of it. One phone call and she'd be here in less than an hour."

Stephanie looked torn. "You know Blake is sorry he couldn't bring you home himself, don't you? He really didn't have any choice but to stay and wrap up his case. There were a zillion more questions he had to answer for the police, not to mention the insurance company."

"I understand. I'm grateful to him for arranging for me to answer the questions they had for me so quickly this morning, so that I could come back to Atlanta this afternoon. And it was incredibly kind of Jeremy to lend us his private plane."

"They both knew you were anxious to get home and check on everything here. And Jeremy thought it would be too uncomfortable for you to ride in a car for very long. He's a really thoughtful guy."

Tara held onto her smile with an effort. "Yes, he is. You and Blake are lucky to have him for a friend."

"He's your friend, too, now. He said so. And Jeremy doesn't take friendship lightly, Tara. None of us do."

"Neither do I, Stephanie. I'll never forget how kind you've all been to me."

"You're sure there's nothing else I can do?"

Tara shook her head. "Call a cab," she urged. "One should be here within fifteen minutes. I'm going to take another pain pill and head straight for bed—my own bed," she added with forced enthusiasm.

Stephanie left reluctantly. "If you need anything...anything at all..."

"I'll call," Tara promised. "Thank you again, Stephanie. For everything."

Stephanie kissed her cheek. "Take care."

"I will."

"I'm sure Blake will be here as soon as he can."

"Stop apologizing for Blake. He can speak for himself," Tara said, trying to sound teasing.

Stephanie didn't smile. "Just…be patient with him, okay? He's never been in love before."

Tara's smile wavered, but she didn't want to argue just then. "Goodbye, Stephanie," she said.

"Not goodbye. See you later," the other woman corrected her. And with that, she finally made her departure, leaving Tara alone for the first time in days.

Tara sighed and rested her head against the back of her couch. It was so quiet in her apartment, she thought. It felt so strange to be back here and not to be afraid that someone was looking for her.

It was even stranger to realize that she'd left her heart back in Savannah with a man who simply hadn't known what to do with it.

She knew Blake had no choice but to remain behind when she left. He had a job to do, a case to finish.

He would always have another case. Another puzzle to solve. Another excuse for living in the shadows under assumed names and identities.

He was very good at his job. It was Blake who'd quietly gathered enough evidence for Doren to be charged with attempted murder, attempted kidnapping, assault, and who knew what else. Blake who'd found the supposedly stolen paintings hidden in Willfort's house, who'd provided proof that Liz Pryce, Willfort's clandestine lover for many years, had sold him the paintings for an exorbitant amount even though she'd suspected at the time that they were fakes.

Apparently, Liz Pryce had confessed the truth to Willfort when she'd learned of his plans to put the artwork on public display. He'd been furious enough with her to break off their relationship, but under threat of her going public and ruining his family-man political image, he'd agreed to keep quiet.

Willfort hadn't been willing to risk having the paintings disclosed as fakes, however. He had his reputation as an art collector to consider—though Blake had said to Tara that Willfort was more of an art-connoisseur-wannabe than a true expert in the field. And, besides, he'd added, Willfort had been infuriated at the possibility that word would get out that he'd been so roundly duped by the woman with whom he'd been having an affair.

And so, Jackson Willfort had come up with the plan to report the paintings stolen. It might even have worked, had Botkin—a man with a great deal of bitterness and a private reason to want reprisal against Liz Pryce and Jackson Willfort—not found out the truth.

Afraid of making the accusation publicly, Botkin had contacted Blake, posing as an agent from the insurance company that carried the policy on the stolen paintings. Since Blake had conducted some investigations for the same company on several previous cases, a couple of which had involved the art gallery in minor ways, it hadn't been too difficult for Botkin to learn how to contact him. But Doren—one of Willfort's personal and well-paid lackeys—had found out about the plan at the last minute, and had taken it upon himself to rush to his boss's defense. Willfort swore he hadn't known about the botched attempted murder.

Tara was still incredibly relieved that Botkin had survived. It seemed that Doren had gotten careless in his panic over Tara and Blake's escape. He and his partner—the man who'd shot at Tara and Blake as they'd run from the gallery—had dumped Botkin's body on the side of a little-used road on their way to search Tara's apartment. They'd apparently believed him to be dead. They'd been wrong—though not by much.

Had a couple of teenagers looking for a make-out spot not happened by only minutes after Doren had driven away, Botkin would have died there on that weed-choked side road. It had been several days before he'd been stable enough to tell the police what had happened to him.

And that, Tara thought with a groan, was something else she was holding against Blake. On Monday evening, when Tara was so upset that she'd been enjoying herself with Jeremy so soon after witnessing what she believed to be a man's murder, Blake had known that Botkin had survived. And he hadn't said a word to her—then, or at any time during the four days that passed before she finally learned the truth.

When she'd asked Blake why he hadn't told her, he'd given her vague explanations about Botkin being in such critical condition that he hadn't been expected to survive the week. He hadn't wanted to get Tara's hopes up only to have her upset again if Botkin died, he'd said. And besides, Botkin would be in even more danger if word should somehow get back to Doren that he was still alive. The fewer people who knew the truth, the safer the man had been.

She hadn't been satisfied with his reasons, but she'd let it drop. There hadn't been time to tell him exactly how she felt about being kept in the dark about so many things.

Tara had actually talked very little with Blake since Doren had grabbed her backstage last night. And all he'd done when they were together was to fill her in on the details of the case, as if nothing at all personal had passed between them during that week together.

They hadn't even spent the night together. Claiming he still had loose ends to tie up, Blake had left Tara in his sister's care after he'd been reassured that Tara wasn't seriously injured. He hadn't even seen her off when she'd left Savannah on Jeremy's private plane this morning. He'd told her goodbye on the telephone, his voice as stilted and polite as if he was talking to a mere passing acquaintance.

He'd broken her heart as painfully as Doren had broken her arm.

Realizing she was crying, Tara dashed angrily at her wet cheeks. She expected to shed many tears over Blake, but she wasn't ready to begin just yet. Her telephone rang and she considered letting the machine pick it up. But then she answered it, instead, deciding that she could use the distraction.

"How are you?"

Blake's deep voice almost started the tears up again, but Tara fought them back. "I'm okay. Stephanie left a few minutes ago, and I was just thinking about taking a pill and going to bed for a while."

"Sounds like a good idea. Are you in much pain?"

"No. Not really," she fibbed, shifting her arm.

"I don't like the thought of you being alone there. Would you like me to call your mom for you? Maybe you should have reconsidered her request for you to spend a few days with her—Jeremy was just as willing to deliver you to your mom's house as to your apartment."

"I really wanted to come home. My own home," she replied, her voice as carefully controlled as his. "And I'm perfectly capable of calling someone if I want company."

"Tara, I—" He paused for what seemed like a long time before speaking again. "I have a new case," he said finally. "I need to start immediately. I'll be out of the state for a while."

It hurt, so badly she had to close her eyes and struggle for composure before she could reply. "Good luck with it," was all she said.

"If you need anything—anything at all—just call Stephanie, okay? She usually knows how to reach me in an emergency."

"I'm sure I'll be fine."

"I'll, er, call you when I'm back in town, okay? We'll talk then."

"You're always promising to talk later, but it never seems to happen, does it? There will always be an excuse. Another case. Something else to hide behind. I think—I think it would be better if you didn't call me again."

Her words seemed to echo hauntingly through the telephone lines.

"Tara, I—"

"I'm afraid I would never be content with what little you're willing to share of yourself, Blake. And I won't resort to dragging reluctant answers out of you one question at a time. I've already tried that. I found it very uncomfortable."

She thought she heard him swallow. "I'm sorry," he said quietly. "I wish...well, I wish I could offer everything you deserve. But I can't. I don't know how."

He sounded weary. Defeated. But instead of feeling sorry for him, she got angry. "You know how, Blake," she disputed. "You just weren't willing to try."

She sensed that he wanted to argue with her. But all he said was, "You'll be all right?"

"I'll be fine," she said, lifting her chin and trying to make herself believe it. "Whatever impression you might have gotten last week, I'm not a quitter. I just needed some time to regroup. I'm going to start looking for a new position immediately."

"You'll find one, if that's what you want. There's nothing you can't do, Tara."

Except make you love me. She swallowed those words and settled for a simple, "Goodbye, Blake. Take care of yourself."

"That's what I'm best at," he replied with a hint of bitterness in his voice.

"For what it's worth," she added quickly, "I don't have any regrets. It wasn't all fun—but it was definitely interesting."

"Tara—"

"I think you're a very special man, Blake. And whatever it is that keeps you moving from place to place, always alone, never able to really share yourself with anyone—whatever it is you're looking for—well, I hope you find it someday. I'm only sorry you couldn't find it with me."

"Tara," he said again, and this time there was a catch in his voice.

She hung up quickly, instantly regretting her impulsive words, knowing she'd revealed much more than she'd intended. She half expected the phone to ring again immediately, for Blake to try to convince her that she was better off without him, or some such nonsense to ease his conscience.

He didn't call back.

Tara drew a long, deep breath, dried her eyes and reached for her pain pills. Just one more brief escape into oblivion before she had to face reality, she promised herself. When she woke up, she had some calls to make.

Blake might be content to spend his life hiding from whatever demons drove him. Tara refused to follow his example.

SEVEN WEEKS LATER, Tara sat once again on the couch in her living room. A pile of file folders and computer printouts were scattered across the coffee table in front of her, along with two rapidly cooling cups of coffee, a half dozen pencils, two calculators and a laptop computer.

"There's no doubt that Mr. Washington has a case," she said, rubbing her temple with one finger. "This is obviously an IRS mistake. He should in no way be responsible for all these penalties and interest."

"That's what I told him." The plump, pleasant-looking woman sitting next to her smiled in satisfaction. "Looks like we've got ourselves a new client, partner."

Tara smiled weakly. "Bringing the number to a grand total of three."

"Hey, we knew we'd have to start slow, right?"

"Right." Tara tossed her pencil onto the table and flexed her left arm, which was still a bit stiff after the weeks in the cast. "Want me to freshen your coffee?"

"Sounds good." Carmen Reyes began to gather papers as she spoke, shuffling them into neat stacks that she stowed in an inexpensive briefcase. "I hope our new office will be ready on Monday like they promised. I don't know about you, but I'm ready to work at a real desk for a change instead of in your living room or at my kitchen table."

Tara smiled. "Me, too. Who would have believed it would take so long just to paint a few..."

She was interrupted by the sudden chime of her doorbell. Her eyebrows rose. She wasn't expecting anyone at this hour on a Saturday morning.

And then someone began to tap on the door. A recognizable rhythm. Shave and a haircut—two bits.

She could almost feel the blood drain from her face. "Oh, God."

Carmen was instantly on her feet. "Tara? What's wrong?"

Smiling a weak reassurance at her friend and new business associate, Tara crossed slowly to the door. She had to brace herself for a moment before she could open it.

Dressed in a pale yellow shirt, baggy gray slacks and black suspenders, his gray felt fedora tilted to a cocky angle on his golden head, Blake held a single, dazzlingly red rose in his right hand. His bright blue eyes went immediately to her hair, which was still a bold, dark red, but he didn't comment.

"Got any coffee?" he asked, his expression unreadable.

She stepped back to let him in. She didn't try to speak yet; she couldn't trust her voice not to break.

Blake smiled at the dark-haired, dark-eyed, olive-skinned woman who had stepped protectively to Tara's side, sensing Tara's distress. "Hello," he said. "I'm Blake Fox."

Tara blinked. Blake *Fox?* Was that his real name, or just another one he'd pulled out of the air? And then she remembered his tattoo, and she thought that maybe this time he'd spoken the truth.

Carmen studied him with the wary eyes of a woman who'd had all too much experience with charming, good-looking men. "Carmen Reyes. Tara's law partner."

Blake's left eyebrow rose. He turned to Tara. "Law partner?"

She nodded, finally finding her voice. "We've just opened our own law firm. I'm tired of fighting the IRS on behalf of huge, wealthy corporations. It has occurred to me that ordinary citizens sometimes get shafted by the system, too. Carmen and I met a few years ago through a professional organization and when she found out I was available, she called and asked if I was interested in going into business with her."

Blake nodded thoughtfully. "It sounds ideal for you," he said simply.

Tara turned to Carmen then. "I know you have plans for the evening. We're finished for the day, aren't we?"

Carmen nodded, looking doubtfully from Tara to Blake. "You don't need me to stay?"

"No. Blake is an old...friend."

Carmen glanced at the rose. "Mmm-hmm."

"It was nice to meet you," Blake told Carmen as she left. "We'll be seeing each other again."

"Will we?" Carmen murmured, looking one more time at Tara before stepping out the door. "I suppose that remains to be seen."

Tara closed the door behind her partner and then smoothed her palms down the legs of the navy slacks she wore with a short-sleeved cream sweater. At least this time Blake hadn't caught her looking grubby and hopeless, she thought with a fleeting sense of relief.

Blake offered the rose. "This is for you."

She took it carefully, as though worried about hidden thorns. "Thank you."

"Your hair is still red. I'd have expected the color to wash out by now."

"It did. I had it dyed again. I like it red."

"So do I. Er...how's your arm?"

"It's fine. The cast has been gone for a week."

"No lingering pain?"

"No. Is that why you're here, Blake?" she asked, deciding not to waste any more time playing games. "Did you suddenly feel the need to make sure that I'm all right? I am, you know."

"I can see that. A new look. A new job. What else has changed?"

"I have," she answered simply. "I'm doing what I want to do now, not what everyone else expects me to do. My new career won't be high-powered or prestigious, and I won't make the money I'd have made in corporate tax law, but I think I'm going to be much happier doing it."

"Good for you. I never had any doubt that you would land on your feet, Tara. That you would find what you wanted."

She nodded, looking down at the rose to hide her expression—afraid that it would reveal that the one thing she'd wanted most was the one thing she hadn't been able to get.

"Now that you've satisfied yourself that I'm all right, there's no need for you to hang around," she said, abandoning her manners for the sake of her pride. She really didn't want to fall apart in front of him, and she was afraid that the longer he remained, the greater would be her chances of doing so.

"There's something I need to tell you before I go."

She steeled herself. "What is it?"

He drew a deep breath. "My last name is Fox," he said. "That's the real one. Stephanie uses it, too. Our parents were carnies—circus performers. We grew up on the road, both of us part of the act by the time we could walk. My parents died when a heavy piece of equipment crashed down on them while they were setting up for a performance. I've blamed myself ever since, because I was supposed to be there to help them, but instead I was off flirting with a pretty tightrope walker."

His mother had survived the accident, only to die a few days later in a hospital, Tara remembered him saying. She reached out to him, laying her hand on his arm, aching for the pain he must have suffered being orphaned so young—and blaming himself. "I'm so sorry. I—"

He shook his head and kept talking, as though he had prepared this speech and was determined to deliver it. "I raised Stephanie on the road, supporting us by working the carnival circuits until she was eighteen. We stayed on the move, sheltered by our carnie friends who knew child-protection services would take Stephanie away from me if they ever caught up with us. I never finished high school, though I made sure Stephanie did—even if she had to change schools at least a dozen times before she finished. I wanted to send her to college, but she already had show business in her blood. She went to work for Jeremy right out of school and started getting modeling jobs not long after that. She was completely self-sufficient by the time she was twenty."

"Blake—"

He held up a hand to silence her. "I've never had a real home," he said. "I've never held what some might call a real job. When I was twenty-one, I needed some quick cash and I earned it by sitting on a stakeout for a P.I. in Dallas. I discovered I had an aptitude for the business, and I started training for it.

"I've built a career from word of mouth, taking the

cases that interested me, turning down the ones that didn't. I had the freedom to do that because I had no obligations, no one to provide for except for myself. I've lived for various lengths of time in twenty different states. I've never had a relationship that lasted more than a few months. I've got friends all over the country, but more than half of them don't know my full name. I've never expected to settle down, get married, have kids...never thought I'd be any good at it. And, considering the way I let my parents down, I didn't think I deserved it. When I met you—a Harvard-educated attorney from a respectable, small-town family, a woman who could have any man she wanted—well, I knew I was way out of my league."

She wouldn't cry, Tara thought fiercely. She wouldn't let her suddenly precarious emotions get away from her. She blinked back the tears that threatened to flood her eyes. "Blake—"

"I knew I was all wrong for you," he finished doggedly. "I knew I would do nothing but disrupt your life...and it turned out I was right. I couldn't even take you out to dinner without getting you involved in something dangerous. When Doren had you...when I knew how badly he was hurting you...when I thought for just one sickening moment that he was going to snap your neck...I almost lost it. I've been throwing knives since I was three, and I've never once hesitated in a crunch...until then. I was terrified that I would miss completely. Or that I would hit you. That you would die because of my mistake. And it paralyzed me."

Her fingers tightened on his arm. "Blake, you saved

my life. You and Jeremy together. If it hadn't been for your quick thinking, and your excellent aim, I wouldn't be here now."

He touched her cheek with an unsteady hand. "If you had died, I would have died with you. And no one except my sister has ever meant that much to me before. I didn't know how to deal with that. I stayed away because I couldn't imagine why a woman like you would want to get mixed up with a man like me. I came back because I can't imagine living the rest of my life without you."

"A man like you?" Tara blinked away her tears and smiled mistily up at him. "You mean a man who gave up years of his life to raise his orphaned sister? A man who sacrificed his own education to make sure that she got one. A man who has made a successful career on his own terms. A man who makes friends—good friends—wherever he goes. Who doesn't judge them by their appearance or their circumstances or their life-style."

She caught his hand in hers and held it against her cheek. "You came to me on that Friday afternoon after I'd been abandoned by others I'd trusted because you cared about me. Because you were worried about me. And then, when we got into trouble through circumstances you had no control over, you watched over me, and you saved my life. You believed in me when I no longer believed in myself. And even when you hurt me—when you broke my heart, damn it—you did so because you thought it was best for me. I don't know whether to hit you or hug you for being so incredibly dense."

"I love you, Tara. I've loved you for so long that you've become a part of me."

"And I've loved you since the first time you stopped by my desk, introduced yourself and told me a really corny joke," she answered.

His eyes closed for a moment. They looked even brighter than usual when he opened them again. "I don't deserve you, Tara McBride. But I'm going to spend the rest of my life making you happy."

"I don't need you to make me happy. I can do that for myself. I only need you to love me."

"Forever," he promised, sweeping her into his arms. "Always."

She locked her arms around his neck. "I won't tie you down, Blake. I have my own career, my own goals. So you keep chasing clues and solving puzzles, whatever it is you enjoy doing. But when you're finished, when you find your answers, you come home to me."

"Actually, I'm thinking about making a few career adjustments of my own," he murmured against her lips. "I think it's time I opened a real office, establish more regular office hours. Private investigation these days is done as often through a computer as through a pair of binoculars. I need a home. An identity. A family. A life."

"That sounds a lot like a marriage proposal," she whispered, almost afraid to hope.

His smile was sheepish. "Not exactly poetic, was it? But it came from my heart. Is it too soon to ask?"

"Oh, Blake." She finally stopped fighting the tears, letting them slide unchecked down her cheeks. "What took you so long?"

"That had better be a yes."

"That's exactly what it is. I love you, Blake Fox."

He crushed her mouth beneath his. And then he bent down to sweep her high against his chest. His hat fell to the carpet, unnoticed, his thick golden hair tumbling boyishly onto his forehead.

"Remember what I said about taking pleasure where you can find it?" he asked.

"Mmm. Are you going to juggle for me?"

A wicked smile slashed across his face. "Eventually."

She really loved it when Blake carried her to bed, Tara thought happily. She looked forward to having him do so for many years to come.

One thing about life with Blake—it would never be boring.

She had so many more questions to ask him. So many things she wanted to tell him about herself. But they could wait.

For now, she was taking her pleasure where she could find it. And she would always find it with Blake, she thought as he tumbled her onto her bed and immediately followed her down.

It's hot...
and it's out of control!

It's a two-alarm Blaze—
from one of Temptation's newest authors!

This spring, Temptation turns up the heat. Look for these bold, provocative, _ultra_-sexy books!

#679 PRIVATE PLEASURES
Janelle Denison
April 1998

Mariah Stevens wanted a husband. Grey Nichols
wanted a lover. But Mariah was determined.
For better or worse, there would be no more private
pleasures for Grey without a public ceremony.

#682 PRIVATE FANTASIES
Janelle Denison
May 1998

For Jade Stevens, Kyle was the man of her dreams. He
seemed to know her every desire—in bed and out. Little
did she know that he'd come across her book of private
fantasies—or that he intended to make every one come true!

BLAZE! Red-hot reads from Temptation!

THE MEN OF BACHELOR CREEK

Alaska. A place where men could be men—and women were scarce!

To Tanner, Joe and Hawk, Alaska was the final frontier. They'd gone to the ends of the earth to flee the one thing they all feared—MATRIMONY. Little did they know that three intrepid heroines would brave the wilds to "save" them from their lonely bachelor existences.

Enjoy

**#662 CAUGHT UNDER
THE MISTLETOE!**
December 1997

#670 DODGING CUPID'S ARROW!
February 1998

#678 STRUCK BY SPRING FEVER!
April 1998

by Kate Hoffmann

Available wherever Harlequin books are sold.

HARLEQUIN® *Temptation*

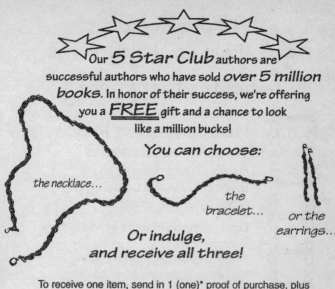

 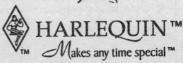